BONES, BULLETS
AND BADMEN

BONES, BULLETS AND BADMEN

by

Link Hullar

Dales Large Print Books
Long Preston, North Yorkshire,
BD23 4ND, England.

British Library Cataloguing in Publication Data.

Hullar, Link
    Bones, bullets and badmen.

    A catalogue record of this book is
    available from the British Library

    ISBN   978-1-84262-772-3 pbk

First published in Great Britain in 1994 by
Robert Hale Limited

Published in Large Print 2010 by arrangement with
Link Hullar care of David Whitehead

Dales Large Print is an imprint of Library Magna Books Ltd.

Printed and bound in Great Britain by
T.J. (International) Ltd., Cornwall, PL28 8RW

For Lane Eric Hullar
and
Willaim Colt MacDonald

ONE

Pete Bates shifted his rangy frame about in an effort to find some comfort from the worn, patched leather saddle. Stiff joints gave off audible snaps as the old man found a new position upon the sturdy, mud-brown gelding. Oblivious to his owner, the big mount simply continued to munch at a stray weed as Bates built a smoke while staring off across the stretch of range he called home.

'Looks like we got us some company,' the rancher spoke to his horse as the animal continued to worry the small green sprout sticking up from the hard-packed earth. Straining to see through the dust cloud that hung upon the distant horizon, the wrinkles around his eyes deepened as the mounted figure squinted in order to follow the approach of the riders across the flat Kansas plains. A dirty thumbnail scratched a Lucifer to flame. Peter Bates puffed the tobacco to life then let his claw-like right hand fall toward the hardwood grip of an old Smith and Wesson Schofield .45 that rested in the holster strapped about his lean waist. A wary grin played about the thin, withered lips while the grey eyes showed growing concern. The spindly fingers of his left hand absently scratched at bristly salt and pepper whiskers upon a lantern jaw as he puffed at the stubby cigarette jutting from the corner of his mouth.

'Wonder what them fellers is wantin' away out here?' Bates mumbled to himself through a cloud of blue smoke. His wrinkled brow furrowed with curiosity. 'Ain't had nothin' to do with any of them boys for goin' on ten years or more.' His fingers brushed the worn grip of the well-oiled .45 and his eyes remained fixed upon the tight cluster of riders while his mind drifted to the wild days.

Pete Bates had done it all in his younger days – including a brief stretch on the owlhoot trail. As a young man following the big war, he had, in turn, rode with rustlers, night raiders, bandits, and a variety of rebel die-hards who refused to admit defeat at the hands of the 'Yankee invaders'. For over a year he had been a part of the infamous Briscoe brothers gang down in Texas. A bloody spree of daring bank jobs and stage coach robberies had convinced Bates that he had signed on for the wrong line of work. He had slipped away from the Briscoes in the dead of night before drifting north and east. Over ten years ago the hardcase rider had wandered into Western Kansas with nowhere else to go. The old owlhoot had remained settled on a small parcel of grazing land from that day to the present. He ran a few head of beef and lived the quiet life of a small rancher. Times had been hard, but Bates had found it to be a good life as well. Now, his past was riding toward him across the dusty prairie. Tall, lanky, tough, and weathered, Pete Bates sat his steady mount to await the arrival of the rough and tumble crew now approaching at a rapid pace. He could recognize trouble riding hard and fast. He knew better than to run.

Bates knew the lead rider immediately. Even at a distance, 'Bad Eye' Bill Malone's hulking presence could be easily identified. The Kansas rancher had first met the veteran outlaw during the time he had ridden with the Briscoes. Even these infamous brothers had not wanted the violent, homicidal brute in their bandit troop, so Malone had gone his separate way to assemble his own small gang of killers and cut-throats. Some years earlier, the big man had lost an eye in a barroom brawl, killing two other men in the process, so he now wore a black, leather patch over the vacant left socket. At five feet and ten inches in height, the notorious hardcase was chunky, solid, and hard-as-nails.

As Malone wrenched back on the reins to pull his spotted mare to a halt, Bates could see a leering grin animate the man's flat face. Quickly the weathered old rancher measured Malone's features. The broken nose and good hazel eye sat under sandy hair and bushy brows of similar shade. Dressed in typical cowboy gear that included a stained grey Stetson, the Remington Frontier .45 sitting high upon his right hip looked as if it had grown there as naturally as any other appendage. Everything about the man seemed vulgar and dirty. Menace radiated from that hazel orb that now fixed upon the leathery face of the rancher with a cold stare.

'Afternoon, Bill.' Bates spoke in an easy manner that belied the knot of fear slowly tightening in his stomach. 'What brings you and the boys to these here parts?'

'You do, Pete.' Malone's hazel eye bored into the older man's skull. Bates became very still as he let his eyes roam over the other four riders sitting their mounts in silence.

Len Holt sat a few feet to Malone's right. He was, next to 'Bad Eye' Bill, the most dangerous of the men before him. While Pete had never met the man, he knew of him from the bloody reputation he had acquired during the years of riding with Malone's outfit. Holt stood only a few inches over five feet and could weigh no more than a hundred and fifteen pounds. However, the two short-barrel Colt .45 revolvers that rode comfortably about the little man's waist were known to be used with fast, deadly accuracy. Clean shaven and handsome, with straight, coal-black hair, the soft spoken young man served as Malone's second in command. Len Holt never strayed far from the side of the big outlaw. The two of them made a formidable team. Holt's expression seemed bored, but Bates was not fooled. He knew that the small man enjoyed killing; Holt's reputation implied a sadistic pleasure from inflicting pain and death. Peter Bates kept a wary eye upon the gunman. His grey eyes shifted between the bandit leader and the petite shootist.

'Can't imagine what you'd be wantin' with a burned out old owlhoot such as me, Bill.' Pete forced a grin that did not travel as far as his eyes. He exhaled a cloud of smoke before flipping the tobacco stub to the ground with his left hand. His right rested upon his thigh near the old pistol's grip. 'Hell, I ain't been in your line of work fer quite some time now.'

The other three riders did not speak. They were typical of the outlaw breed. Worn cowboy clothing, dishevelled and patched, covered husky, powerful frames. By and large, their features evidenced stubble sketched chins, stringy, unkempt hair, and a variety of scars as proof to the hard and violent lives they had so far survived. Wide brimmed hats gave shade and masked faces in shadows. These three hardcases were widely spread behind their two leaders, Malone and Holt.

'You got somethin' that we want,' the diminutive Holt spoke for the first time in icy, soft tones.

'I ain't got nothin' here but an old ranch shack and a couple hundred head of beef.' The old man shook his head in bewilderment. 'Hell, Bill, I just barely get by with enough to keep beans on the table!'

'What we want is in your head, Pete.' Malone's leering grin broke into a wide smile that exposed yellow, cracked stubs that passed for teeth. Greed animated the rugged features of the outlaw boss. 'You just tell us what we want to know and we'll be on our way quick as you please.'

'I just can't foller where you're headed fer, Bill.' Bates fumbled for words while he stalled for time. Fear ate away at his insides. Slowly, he was coming to understand what it was that Malone wanted and, just as slowly, he came to realize that he was about to die. 'Ain't nothin' that I can do fer you, Bill. I've been out of circulation fer a long, long time and...'

BOOM!

Without warning, before the Kansas rancher even knew what was happening, he felt the force of a numbing blow to his right shoulder as the .45 slug punched a hole through his body. The impact of the bullet knocked the lanky figure from his saddle. He crashed to the earth while his frightened

16

horse pranced away in wide-eyed fear.

Len Holt's pistol was back in the holster almost before Bates hit the ground; his right hand no more than a blur of speed. The gunman looked down upon the figure sprawled before his pinto pony. As the rancher writhed in agony, Len Holt's eyes sparkled with delight. For the first time, the little man seemed to come alive in the warm afternoon sunlight.

Bill Malone grunted as he stepped down from the saddle. He slowly closed the gap that separated him from the prone figure of Pete Bates, then removed the man's revolver to stuff it into the belt of his own frayed green trousers.

'You won't be needin' this, Pete.' Malone grinned as Bates struggled to sit up. Strong, bony fingers wrapped in leather-like skin grasped his right shoulder while the arm hung limp and useless. Crimson flowed through the grip his left hand had upon the wound, making a small puddle upon the dusty prairie beneath him. The rancher's grey eyes reflected both his pain and his fear.

'Ain't no cause fer all this, Bill.' In spite of his wound, Bates managed to make his voice sound strong as he attempted to bluff it out. 'You know if I could help out that I'd be more'n happy to...'

A small boot caught the older man on his left cheek, opening the skin to the bone. The kick sent blood dripping onto the dirty, stained shirt front that hung about his shallow chest while propelling the figure back to the flat, hard ground from which he had struggled to a sitting position just moments before. Holt had dismounted close behind Malone. Kicking out with his right boot, the gunman had quickly silenced the wounded man.

'We mean business, old man.' Holt's eyes shone with pleasure. 'So far you've just had a sample of the pain I can provide if you don't tell us where to find that payroll.'

There it was. Pete Bates had known what Malone must want, but now it was out in the open with no way to avoid it. The massacre of those federal troops had been the final undoing of the Briscoe brothers and the last outlaw job before Bates had set out on the drift. Too much money and too many dead men to his liking; even after all these years the memory haunted his dreams. Somehow, Pete Bates had always known this day would come in some form or another.

'Now, Len here, he don't know you like I do, Pete.' Malone knelt beside the wounded rancher. 'I mean, me and you go way back. I wouldn't want to see nothin' happen to you now old partner, but I can't be responsible for what my friend here might do if you don't cooperate on the matter of that there federal payroll shipment.' The outlaw chief's grin bespoke cruel possibilities while Holt looked on with undisguised interest. 'You're the one that'll have to decide just how long this here is gonna take.'

'Honest, I just don't know...' Bates began a hastily constructed explanation with desperation apparent in his voice, while pain and terror battled for control of his face.

BOOM!

The small man's left-hand .45 interrupted the rancher's feeble attempt at a story. The lead ploughed through the meaty portion of the old outlaw's left thigh, and a stream of scarlet poured forth to create a thick, muddy design in the heavy dust of the Kansas prairie. As Bates groaned in pain, Holt slid the pistol home in the holster strapped about his waist. The gunman looked on with obvious anticipation.

'Your call, Pete.' Malone licked dry cracked lips without blinking an eye. 'You know what it is we want to know. All you got to do to end this here standoff is to tell us where we can find that missing stash of treasure.'

'Long time ago, Bill...' Bates gasped out the words through pain clenched teeth, 'can't rightly recollect just where it was we...'

BOOM!

Another shot sounded that brought a sharp cry of surprised pain from the bleeding man. Bates lay helpless upon the hard earth with a third hole leaking crimson; this one high in his right thigh. Each of the wounds had been well placed to inflict pain by punching holes through flesh and muscle while avoiding bones and vital organs. While the blood flowed freely, the tough, weathered rancher might still survive the brutal attack if properly cared for by a competent physician.

'Gawd, Bill...' Bates screamed with the agony of his wounds. His grey eyes begged for relief, but encountered only amused contempt in the hazel eye of Bill Malone. The scream turned to a low groan as the Kansas cattleman again gritted his teeth against the throbbing in this legs and shoulder. His battered old frame could not take much more.

'Think real hard, Pete.' Malone smiled again with his face just inches from that of the other man. Bates could feel his warm, foul breath upon his cheeks. 'Back in the old Reconstruction days just after the war. The damn Yankees were runnin' things down in Texas when you and them Briscoe brothers knocked over a federal payroll up in the Panhandle. You boys shot up a bunch of cavalry soldiers from ambush, then made off with a heap of gold, silver, and federal bills. Nobody ever found that treasure, Pete. That payroll was stashed away for the Briscoes, but they weren't lucky enough to spend it. Seems old Willy and Dalton Briscoe went out dancin' from the gallows just a few months later. Now, all you've got to do is tell me where it is you helped the Briscoes hide all that Yankee loot. Tell old Bill what you know and all this here pain will be behind you.'

'I'm tellin' you, Bill, I just don't know!'

'Len!' Malone bellowed in frustration. In response, Holt slowly and deliberately withdrew a pistol from his holster to level the weapon upon the fallen man's left shoulder. His finger began to tighten upon the trigger as his eyes met those of his victim sprawled upon the ground.

'No!' Bates let loose a frightened shout that filled the air. 'I'll tell you what I know. I swear it, Bill. Don't let him shoot me again.' He shifted his eyes from Holt to Malone. The one-eyed bandit remained kneeling by the rancher's side on the hard prairie earth. 'I'll tell it all,' Bates pleaded with the outlaw boss, 'just keep that crazy killer away from me.'

'Don't hold out on us, Pete.' Malone spoke with quiet assurance while Holt held the revolver steady upon the weakened figure of the bleeding cattleman.

'As best I can recollect…' Pete's voice was growing raspy and weak as the life fluid leaked from his rangy frame. His mind seemed to be slipping as he fumbled for words. 'It seems that the closest town was a little place called Spit Junction, just south of Palo Duro Canyon down in the Texas Panhandle region.' His mouth hung slack while his grey eyes began to glaze over.

'Go on, Pete,' Malone slapped the be-whiskered face a stinging blow while urging the man on, 'tell us the rest.'

'My head's all fuzzy,' Bates complained. 'I can't seem to get it all together. Maybe a stiff shot would brace me, Bill; just one shot of whiskey.'

'Later,' Malone lied, 'just tell me where you all hid the loot and I'll give you anything you want.'

'I just can't get my mind wrapped around it … if only I could have a…'

BOOM!

Holt fired once more. The heavy slug shattered the man's left shoulder. Bates bellowed in pain, shock, and anger. This time the gunman had struck bone as well as flesh. Already in serious condition, this final shot would do the rancher in for good.

'What the hell're you doin' Len?' queried Malone with a disgruntled glare. 'He's tellin' us what he knows.'

'I just want to make sure he tells it straight,' the little man answered in a quiet, flat voice. His eyes betrayed the joy he took in the wounded man's suffering.

'Put that damn pistol away!' Bill Malone spoke with authority and Holt let the revolver slide home with a shrug of his narrow shoulders.

As Malone shifted his attention back to

the figure before him, he could see that Pete Bates was dying. Scarlet flowed freely from the four bullet wounds, and the tough old rancher would not last much longer.

'Come on now, Pete!' the outlaw chief implored. 'You tell us where to find that loot from the payroll and we'll treat you right. Why we'll patch you up and have you on your feet in no time. What do you say, Pete?'

'Texas Panhandle … Spit Junction … closest town to the treasure…' thin, withered lips turned up in a final, triumphant grin, 'you'll never find it.' Pete Bates closed his eyes as his body shook with a final death rattle, then lay limp and still upon the muddy, red earth.

'Damn!' Malone let the rancher's head fall to the ground with a heavy thud. He turned upon the gunman standing a few feet behind him. 'You had to go and kill him. You just had to put your fun ahead of our business!'

'We know where to start looking anyway.' Holt turned as he spoke. Quickly, he paced off the distance to his pinto and remounted without another word.

'Bad Eye' Malone trudged back to his own mount with a scowling visage. He pulled himself into the saddle then heaved a deep sigh before addressing the other riders who now surrounded him. All eyes focused upon their leader as they awaited further instructions.

'Okay, boys,' Malone growled at his followers, 'let's make tracks for Texas.'

Without another word, the five hardcase riders set off south and west toward the Lone Star state. Pete Bates lay dead upon the prairie. His worst nightmare had taken more than ten years to become a reality. The past had a way of catching up with everyone – sooner or later.

Several nights later, many miles away, in the flat, arid plains of the Texas Panhandle, an old mountain man unfurled a tattered bedroll beneath the stars. He settled weary bones beside a small blaze in the chill of the spring evening. He was tired. It had been a long day. Seventy-odd years of living wore heavy on a man by the time the sun sank beneath the horizon; even a leather tough old figure such as the one that now stretched his long frame out upon the soiled blanket to sigh in contentment.

William 'Three Toes' Russell was one of the last of the mountain men who had come early to the far west and remained. Buckskins covered the old man's figure while his feet were shod in moccasins. A bushy grey beard masked the lower face, with long hair of similar shade braided into a tail that hung halfway down the man's back. Eyes as green as a summer meadow were sharp and clear. Wrinkled leather made up the little skin that could be seen on the old frontiersman's face and hands. However, anyone could see from the quick, agile movements that the man maintained a cat-like quality to his muscles. An active, outdoor life kept the old man healthy, limber, and strong.

His wiry, five and a half foot frame uncoiled upon the frayed blanket as the mountain man began removing items from his person in order to get comfortable for the night. First, he slipped a patched worn cap of indescribably mixed furs from his iron grey head. Next, he pulled a Bowie blade from his belt, along with a sharp-edged tomahawk. Unbuckling his cartridge belt, Russell gently laid the holstered Smith and Wesson American .44 beside his bedroll. The ornate pistol was his pride and joy. Finally, before drifting off to sleep, Three Toes reached out a leathery claw to pat the old Henry .44 that lay within easy reach. There could be little doubt that Russell was ready for any trouble that might come upon him in the dark of night. The real question, the old man grinned to reveal even, white teeth, was whether or not trouble was ready for him.

William Russell had been born in the hills of south eastern Ohio in 1809. He had come west of the Mississippi in 1828 upon the death of his parents. From that time until the present, he had roamed the far western frontier. While he had spent time all around, he returned more and more to the mountains of western Montana Territory. It was here that he had engaged in the early days of the fur trade. After all these years, Three Toes still called these mountains home.

Russell had helped the Texicans win their independence from Mexico before drifting back to the fur trade in the rugged Rocky Mountains. The Mexican War found the veteran frontiersman serving as an army scout in the campaigns against the forces of Santa Anna. Somewhere during his time in the mountains he had been captured by a roving band of Blackfeet Indians and tortured; with the result that he possessed only three toes upon his left foot. Hence the nickname 'Three Toes'.

Over the years, Russell had trapped, traded, served as an army scout, and engaged in almost any type of honorable activity available to a man of independent spirit. Increasingly, as the years wore on, he spent more and more time in his beloved mountains, but occasionally ventured south toward Texas to visit with his old friend, Isaiah 'Bullwhip' Wallace of the Bar W ranch in Croly County, Texas. It was Bullwhip's hospitality that had embraced Russell in the warmth of the Wallace home throughout the winter and early spring. He had been on the trail two weeks now headed steady north and east.

In addition to the fellowship of an old saddle partner, two good things had come from his most recent visit at the Bar W. One stood quietly by in the night. A young, black stallion named Jimmy. Three Toes knew that he could count on the quick, powerful horse for many years of service and companionship. The other, more important development, had been news that another mutual friend was now located in the Texas Panhandle. Armed only with this knowledge, the old mountain man had set off to search out an old gunfighter who had been reported dead a few years earlier. Russell would be glad to see the old shootist. If anyone could track him down, Three Toes knew he was the man for the job. He supposed that his old friend was the snowy side of sixty by now, but he had called him 'son' since their time together during the Mexican War.

It would be good to visit with another old friend. Those who stood beside him during the wild days were growing few and far between. Not much time left to an old mountain lion like him, he thought with a grin. It would be so very good to see Elijah West one last time before he rode back toward the rugged mountains to the Montana Territory to find his cabin safe in the high country. Three Toes smiled a final sleepy grin as he savoured the notion of a joyful reunion over a tall bottle of Tennessee whiskey. He drifted to sleep with the peace of a life well lived.

TWO

William 'Three Toes' Russell tugged lightly upon the reins to bring Jimmy, the big, black stallion, to a halt upon the small ridge he had crested a moment before. Surveying the flat, rugged terrain before him, Russell's keen eyes saw mostly scrubby brush and an occasional long-eared Texas jackrabbit. Focusing his vision upon the well-worn trail that stretched out towards the horizon, he could make out a pair of figures stirring puffs of dust as they trudged steadily in the direction of the nearest town.

'Man afoot in this here territory must be some kind of a fool,' the old mountain man, trapper, and scout muttered under his breath. His expression changed a bit as he scratched at the chin hidden beneath the grey, bushy beard. 'Either a fool or in some kind of trouble.' He gently touched heels to Jimmy who stepped forward to begin their descent from the sharp ridge. Moving at a steady trot, horse and rider easily began to close the gap that separated them from the walking figures of two oddly matched men. Neither of the men, as yet, noticed the approach of the buckskin clad old-timer who sat easily upon the big charcoal.

'I'll be a dagblasted buffler chip!' Russell's voice brought an answering nicker from Jimmy as they came closer to the objects of their concern. His face broke into a wide grin that crinkled the corners of his eyes as Three Toes scratched between the horse's twitching ears and offered another observation.

'If that don't beat all then I ain't an ornery old cuss from the high hills!' He urged the animal forward with another touch of his heels before concluding, 'Which I most certainly am.'

The sight which had brought both grin and exclamation from the old man might have done the same from anyone who encountered these same two pedestrians. The two men who casually proceeded along this Panhandle horse trail were engaged in an intense and animated debate while wearing nothing more than high top boots, pith helmets, and long, red flannel underwear. Russell watched the lively discussion in amused silence as the two figures strolled onward, oblivious to his arrival upon the scene.

'No, no, my dear fellow,' the smaller, older man spoke sharply as he gestured with both arms flailing about, 'you really do have it all backward old boy. Prehistoric man might never have developed the wheel at all without chance occurrence and simple coincidence. Why I have little doubt that...' The man rambled on, but Three Toes stopped listening as he looked the fellow over from head to toe. Around fifty years of age, the frail, little man stood several inches shy of six feet and weighed in at around one hundred pounds. As he spoke, the emaciated figure lifted the pith helmet with the bony fingers of his left hand while wiping perspiration from his hairless dome with the right. A sharp, hawk nose, sunken eyes whose colour was lost in the shadows, and sail-like ears of enormous proportions completed the man's unusual appearance. He wrapped up his argument with a finger pointed toward heaven and a triumphant ring to his squeaky, bird-like voice, 'and there you have it my fine friend, a simple response to your earlier theory.'

'Honestly, my dear, dear colleague,' the other man began his retort, 'I really cannot agree with you. If early man had been dependent upon mere coincidence, then...' The taller figure's voice prattled on while Russell shifted his attention to the younger of the two travellers. Long arms windmilled as the big man spoke and, like his companion, the man was intent upon the discussion they pursued while strolling along in the bright, spring sunshine. Somewhere in his late thirties, the current speaker stood six feet in height and would weigh a solid two hundred pounds. His broad shoulders and deep chest conveyed an impression of strength. However, the thick, horn-rimmed glasses and pale complexion went far to shake that image. Bushy red hair stuck out in all directions while a broad, open face carried a multitude of freckles along with a wide, honest smile. A good natured grin never left the man's countenance even as he spoke. 'I'm afraid, good sir,' he concluded with an amiable shaking of his bushy red head, 'that you simply have not considered all the evidence at your disposal.'

'Now, really dear boy...' the older man began before being interrupted by the man on horseback. The old scout now followed close behind the odd couple in long handles, boots, and pith helmets. He could restrain himself no longer.

'Excuse me, gents,' Russell spoke up in his usual scratchy tone. He made no effort to hide the amusement so evident in his clear, meadow-green eyes. 'Y'all jist out fer a stroll or you goin' some place in particular?'

Startled, both men twirled about in their surprise to find the buckskin clad trapper looking down upon them from the back of Jimmy. A grin animated the old man's features while his eyes sparkled with good humour.

'My goodness, sir,' the older man exclaimed with a mixture of relief and joy, 'a pleasure to make your acquaintance I'm sure, but you gave us both quite a start!'

'Indeed,' agreed the younger companion as he nodded his head to affirm the point. An ear to ear grin served to further enliven the wiry red hair and freckles, making the younger man appear the very soul of happiness.

'Please, allow me to make introductions,' the little figure removed the pith helmet. His hairless dome sparkled as the sun played upon beads of perspiration. 'I am Professor Milton T. Robertson of Hopkins College in Howardville, Maine. My esteemed colleague to my right,' he indicated the younger man beside him with a dramatic gesture of the left hand, 'is Professor Tillery J. Montgomery of the same highly acclaimed institution of higher learning. We are abroad in your fine region in order to examine the fossilized remains of prehistoric animals in an effort to ascertain whether or not said animals might have…'

'Is he all together straight in his head?' Russell turned a puzzled expression upon the younger man whose freckled face beamed upward in a friendly grin.

'Indeed, my good man,' Professor Montgomery began, 'he is simply trying to explain that the study of fossilized animal relics combined with the careful excavation of long buried artifacts from prehistoric man will enable us…'

'Never mind,' Three Toes held up a hand to bring the stream of strange words to a halt as he shook his head in befuddled amazement. Meanwhile, the two eastern professors gazed upon him with polite smiles as if they had not a care in the world. 'Could you tell me in one word what it is you're lookin' fer in these parts?'

'Bones,' Professor Robertson cheerfully responded, 'old, buried bones.'

Russell let his eyes shift to Montgomery as he searched the man's smiling, freckled countenance for verification of the other's answer.

'Quite right, good sir, quite right,' came the ready assurance from the younger man.

Removing the fur cap from his grey head, the old scout scratched at his scalp with an absent-minded gesture as he examined the men standing before him. He leaned forward, then shifted his frame in the saddle in an effort to find a more comfortable position. Satisfied at last, he reached up with his left hand to stroke the bushy beard before speaking again to the professors.

'Jist let me ask you gents another question,' Three Toes spoke with genuine curiosity in his voice.

'Certainly,' the two chorused a cheerful response.

'Do you have to do this in your underwear?'

'No,' Professor Robinson replied with a grin of his own. 'I'm afraid we have met with a small misfortune brought on by a slight miscalculation.'

'Indeed,' Professor Montgomery concurred with a shake of his head, 'a small misfortune that resulted in our own serious error in judgement.' His broad smile provided no hint of annoyance at his current circumstances.

'Either of you care to fill me in on this here "misfortune" You keep rattlin' about?' The old man's grin returned as he listened to the eastern professors. 'It might be that I could help out a bit if only I knew what the trouble was all about.'

'How kind of you to offer, sir,' Robertson replied. 'Don't you think so, Professor?'

'Certainly Professor,' Montgomery assured him, 'so very kind of him to offer.'

Russell simply shook his head in frustrated silence as the two proclaimed his virtues for an additional minute while he waited to hear their tale of misjudgment and misfortune.

'As I have indicated previously,' the older man began, 'I am Professor Milton T. Robertson of Hopkins College in Howardville, Maine and...'

'I've got that part, Milly, jist git on with the rest of it will you?' Three Toes interrupted with a gruff edge to his steady, scratchy voice.

'No, no, that's Professor Milton T....'

'Git on with the story!' the old trapper growled.

'Well, several days ago we connected up with a guide who was to show us about the region so we could locate the area we were seeking. Our goal is the excavation of the remains from prehistoric beasts who freely roamed this territory some...'

'I ain't in need of no history lesson, Milly,'

Russell interrupted him once again as his green eyes flashed the danger signals of impatience, 'jist git on with the tale.'

'Well,' the older professor continued with a good natured grin showing no irritation at the interruption, 'I am afraid we misjudged the guide's moral character, for last night Professor Montgomery and myself went to sleep before a warm fire, only to awaken this morning as you see us now. The guide was gone along with our animals, clothing, and supplies. A small stroke of bad luck I'd say.'

'Yes, yes,' Montgomery smiled in agreement, 'just a small misfortune I'm afraid.'

'Don't you gents understand that you could die out here afoot in this Texas Panhandle country?' The old man shook his head in disbelief. 'Whoever took your animals might jist as well have shot you in the back.'

'Well, I hardly think the matter to be that serious, my dear fellow. There's really no call for you to become so excited.' Robertson's face seemed to rejoice in life. 'We have been making steady progress toward the next town throughout the early morning.'

'Quite right, Professor,' Montgomery bobbed his bushy red head in affirmation. 'By my calculations, we are only some forty odd miles from the village of Spit Junction, Texas.'

'Gents,' Three Toes made every effort to

reply with a steady tone to his voice in order to mask the growing sense of frustration with the two Easterners, 'out here on the high plains, greenhorns sich as you could be stone cold dead afore you walked forty miles to the nearest town. Now, jist lissen to me … uh … uh…' He fumbled for the younger man's name.

'Professor Tillery J. Montgomery of Hopkins College at your service, sir.'

'Now then, lissen to me, Tilly,' Russell raised a hand for silence when the big man with freckled features opened his smiling mouth to correct him regarding his name. 'I want you and Milly there to take a seat over on them boulders you see yonder.' He pointed a gnarled finger in the direction of a small cluster of rocks and scrub brush that would provide minimal shade in the growing heat of mid-morning. Unstrapping one of the canteens from his saddle horn, the trapper continued, 'Take small, slow sips, rest, and argue til you're blue in the face, but I want both of you to wait right there until you see me come back fer you.'

'Where will you be, Mister…' Montgomery accepted the canteen with a grateful face as he wiped a dry tongue across cracked lips. 'I'm sorry, but we never seem to have learned your name.'

'The name's William Russell,' the old mountain man responded. He turned his horse to begin following the back trail left by the professors along the narrow horse path. 'Friends call me Three Toes.' He set out the way he had come with his sharp, green eyes upon the ground as he retraced the morning walk of his new found charges. 'I'll be finding your outfit while you wait here fer me.'

A little less than an hour later, the buckskin clad figure of the old scout and trapper cautiously approached a makeshift camp beside a muddy creek. Holding the big Henry rifle at his waist, he advanced in silence. Years of erosion had eaten away at the plains, so the little stream crawled along the bottom of steeply sloping banks with spindly trees and scrubby brush growing about the water source. On the same side of the murky little stream as Russell, a man hunkered before a canvas pack in the midst of a cluttered, chaotic camp site.

Three Toes had left Jimmy behind, so he walked quietly now as he closed the distance separating him from the man and animals settled near the muddy ribbon of water. Five horses stood spread about at random. Having drunk their fill of the water, they gnawed at stray brush while ignoring the man in their midst who concentrated upon his search of packs and bundles that had been haphazardly dumped upon the earth.

He was a big man. Well over six feet tall and more than two hundred pounds, he had dark hair, cauliflower ears, and an oft-broken nose. A greasy, stained, checkered shirt strained across his broad chest while patched corduroys were tucked into scuffed, stove-pipe boots. An old Starr .44 rested upon his left hip with the grip turned out-ward for a cross draw. Intent upon his search of the canvas bags that lay before him the big man did not hear the wiry figure who approached on careful, moccasined feet.

'I'd jist as soon kill you,' the old man spoke softly as he came to a halt some fifty feet away, 'so don't make no mistakes nor any sudden moves.'

The big man stiffened slightly, then relaxed again while remaining in the squatting position before the items strewn about on the ground. Looking up at the grey-headed old trapper, the broken-nosed face managed a crooked grin.

'Somethin' I can do for you, old man?'

'Fer starters you can fergit the "old man" talk or I'll come over there and slap that silly grin offen your ugly face.'

A scowl quickly replaced the grin, but the big man made no reply as he remained still. His eyes shifted back and forth between the Henry rifle and the steady green eyes that bored through him. Big and ugly made no move towards the .44 strapped about his waist.

'Now,' Three Toes continued, 'you can start packin' all this here stuff up and loadin' them animals.' The man rose slowly to his feet as he stared down the muzzle of the big Henry .44. 'And be damn quick about it, sonny!'

'Hold on a minute now...' Big and ugly began to protest, but his words fell silent as he caught the grim look of determination in those deadly green eyes. Russell's claw-like old hands held the rifle firmly. It was obvious the old man meant business.

'Jist move slow and easy while you git on with the packin'. I've got a lot of ground to cover this afternoon so don't keep me waitin'. You've already taken up too much of my time, boy.'

The man began stuffing items into canvas bags as he shuffled about the camp site collecting scattered supplies. After some twenty minutes of silent labour, under the careful watch of William Russell, the big man had managed to load the horses in a reasonable fashion. Finishing his labours, he turned to face the old trapper once again.

'Now what?' Big and ugly asked with a sneer. 'You don't think I'm gonna just let you ride away with all this loot do you?'

'I don't think you got much of a choice, sonny.'

A gleam of hope burned in the big man's dark eyes. 'You could give me a fair chance; every man deserves a fair chance don't he?'

'Oh sure,' the mountain man's voice dripped with sarcasm. 'Like you give them two college teachers a fair chance when you stole everything they owned and set 'em both afoot here on the plains? You think that deserves a fair chance?'

Big and ugly only kicked at the earth with a scuffed boot toe and scowled.

'But,' Russell heaved an exaggerated sigh, 'I always have been a man with a soft heart and feeble brain, so I suppose even a nasty feller sich as yourself does deserve some kind of a chance.' As Three Toes finished the declaration, he stooped to place the big Henry rifle upon the earth at his feet. Before he could even straighten his frame, big and ugly had the pistol from his holster in a swift, smooth cross draw. A malicious grin distorted his already grotesque features as he levelled the Starr .44 upon the old man's chest.

BOOM!

A look of stunned disbelief washed over the big man's ugly, unshaven face. His pistol grew heavy in the outstretched hand.

BOOM!

Pain twisted his lips as crimson began to leak from his mouth and nostrils while the scarlet stain upon his chest grew even larger. Fingers became numb, his grip loosened, and the big Starr revolver fell to the hard ground, followed shortly by Big and ugly who crumpled to the earth in a sprawling, lifeless heap.

The ornate Smith and Wesson American .44 remained firm in the trapper's grip as he approached the fallen hardcase. A hard, grim look froze the whiskered face.

'I'm old,' he spoke to the corpse at his feet, 'not stupid.'

49

'Jist head on down this here trail and you'll come to Spit Junction by early this evenin'.' Three Toes spoke to the professors who fumbled with the packs strapped to the backs of their horses. Before noon Russell had returned the animals and supplies belonging to Professors Robertson and Montgomery. The men had quickly dressed in tan canvas pants and brown cotton shirts before beginning a quick inspection of their jumbled belongings. 'Now, don't dawdle, gents,' he cautioned. 'Git yourselves in the saddle and push hard fer town afore the day gits away from you.'

'But did you have to kill him, Mr Russell?' Robertson asked with genuine remorse. 'I mean, it is a shame for civilized men to resort to violence and bloodshed. Murder is hardly a solution...'

'We've been all over that ground, Milly,' Russell let his green eyes meet the professor's intense gaze. 'I don't leave unfinished business to haunt my back trail. I didn't live to be this old by leavin' enemies to catch up with me. If I hadn't killed that man, then he'd sure enough have been follerin' behind me, and one of us would have ended up dead. I give him a fair chance to a fair fight but the ornery cuss went fer his gun afore I even had the chance to git set. You know he didn't have to pull that pistol on me. Trouble for him was I expected he'd do jist about what he did and I put darlin' Corey here to work afore he had a chance to pull the trigger.' The scout gave an affectionate pat to the beautiful pistol that rested upon his right hip.

A heavy sigh escaped the professor's lips. He sadly shook his head while his voice quivered in sorrow for the passing of the owlhoot.

'Well,' Robertson spoke softly, 'at least he received a decent burial. That's the least that could be…'

'Burial?' Russell exploded. 'Why I wouldn't waste my time on a sorry hardcase sich as that. He's coyote bait by evenin' and a buzzard banquet by day.' The trapper laughed at his own joke, but the professors were horrified.

'Mr Russell, why surely you don't mean...?' Montgomery began a question while Robertson seemed on the verge of tears.

Three Toes abruptly terminated the conversation by touching heels to Jimmy in order to set off toward the small town of Spit Junction at a quick walk.

'Remember what I told you.' Russell waved a hand as he turned his back upon the two eastern professors. 'Git them horses movin' and push on into town afore dark.'

'Thank you very much, Mr Russell. We do appreciate all you've done for us.' Robertson recovered quickly to call out to the departing figure. 'Our sincere appreciation for your many acts of kindness.'

'Quite so, Mr Russell,' Montgomery echoed the sentiments of his companion, 'thank you, indeed.'

Russell only continued to wave the claw-like hand over his shoulder while urging Jimmy on toward town. He would be there long ahead of the odd Easterners. Furthermore, he hoped to avoid the professors at all times while in town. In fact, it was in Spit Junction where the old mountain man hoped to find a good friend and a bottle of fine Tennessee whiskey. His soul craved a reunion with a kindred spirit while his belly churned for a few jolts of that amber lightning. Spit Junction, Texas should be the place.

THREE

'Ain't much of a town,' William Russell muttered under his breath as the young, black stallion carried him down the dusty trail labelled Main Street. 'Fact is, this looks like the only street in Spit Junction.' The old man's small grin remained hidden by the bushy, grey whiskers.

Faded letters had spelled out the town's name upon a weathered, grey board. A dozen or so residences and a few less commercial buildings were all there appeared to be to the lazy, little Panhandle community. Two saloons, a bank, a two storey hotel, a livery stable, a general mercantile, and a combination hardware store/gunsmith shop seemed to make up the bulk of the business district. All the structures evidenced the worn look of wood baked in the Texas summer sun and then scrubbed by the freezing northern winds that swept through the high plains throughout the winter. A small town such as this would support a variety of ranches and farms scattered throughout the surrounding countryside. Three Toes had seen all of these settlements that he cared to visit over the past fifty years or so. However, this one was different. A friend lived here somewhere along this wide little path called Main Street.

A slight tug on the reins turned Jimmy's head toward the small store labelled HARDWARE AND GUNS; Joshua Easterly, proprietor. A faint grin stirred among the grey bush that dominated the trapper's lived-in face. He stepped down from the saddle to wrap the big black's reins about the hitching post. Patting the animal gently upon the neck, Russell moved lightly to pass through the shop doorway.

An attractive woman, about mid-thirties, stood at the counter. Dressed in a prim, floral print dress, her rounded figure caught the old scout's eye immediately. A pleasant, if not beautiful, face seemed to indicate strength and character while the soft, brown hair, worn tied in a tight bun at the nape of her slender neck, showed strands of silver. The lady was purchasing a small Smith and Wesson Pocket .32, and Russell supposed that Joshua Easterly must be the gentleman offering this customer such very special assistance. In fact, Mr Easterly only let his sky-blue eyes shift briefly to the newcomer before returning his full attention to the attractive woman who stood across the glass display case at the back of the hardware store.

'Be right with you, stranger,' was the only comment the shop owner made.

'No hurry,' Three Toes responded. 'I'll just look around fer what I need.'

The buckskin clad trapper poked through the merchandise all neatly arranged about the small shop. Fingering the usual hardware goods one would expect to find, Russell really used the time to measure the man behind the counter.

Joshua Easterly looked to be a fine figure of a man. Russell judged his age to be about sixty, but he was still a straight, powerful individual who stood over six feet tall and weighed in at more than two hundred pounds. Broad shoulders narrowed to lean hips where a single, old Colt Navy .36 rested in a worn holster upon his right thigh. The walnut grip looked dark and smooth. Thick, silver hair topped his head, but the rugged face was clean shaven. A straight nose and sharp sky-blue eyes dominated the weathered, but not unhandsome features. Simple clothing complimented the big man's strong appearance. A green checked shirt was stuffed into faded jeans; these, in turn, were cuffed above serviceable cattleman's boots.

Indeed, Joshua Easterly was an impressive figure. Even more impressive was the truth. The hardware shop's owner was, in fact, a gunman of legendary proportions.

'Thank you, now, Mrs Shafer,' Easterly offered the woman a pleasant, friendly smile displaying white, even teeth. 'I do hope that pistol will provide you with the security you're lookin' for and, please, do feel free to call upon me if I can be of further assistance.'

'Thank you, Mr Easterly.' A lively grin animated the woman's features as she stepped through the door into the street that fronted the hardware store. Russell watched her cross the dusty trail before turning his meadow-green eyes upon the silver-haired figure behind the counter.

'It's been a while, son.' The old man spoke softly even though they were alone in the store. He approached his old friend with quick, easy steps. 'Fer a while there I thought that you was dead, boy.'

Easterly smiled as he stuck out his hand across the glass counter that held a dozen revolvers. Not many folks called him 'son' and 'boy', but this old friend had done so for over thirty years. Green eyes locked with blue while warm, friendly looks were exchanged with the firm grasp of hard, calloused hands. It was a moment before either man could find his voice.

'I don't kill easy,' the silver-haired man spoke with a hint of a grin playing about his lips.

'That I do believe,' Russell snickered in response as he leaned an elbow upon the gun counter.

'How'd you find me?' The sky-blue eyes carried a level of concern not evident in the words of the simple question.

'No need to worry, son,' the trapper met his gaze to offer up a wink. 'Your secret's safe. I was down visitin' our old partner Bullwhip Wallace at the Bar W. He's the one tipped me off that you was still among the livin' up here on the plains. So, I stopped by on my way back home to the Montana Territory.'

'Glad you did, Three Toes.'

'I don't suppose this here is a good place fer us to visit considerin' you ain't supposed to be who you really is and all that sich a thing.'

'No,' the silver head nodded in agreement, 'but I'll stop by the Emerald Palace Saloon after I lock up tonight to pick up a bottle of the finest Tennessee whiskey in town. After I leave there, you come around to the back of this building, knock on the door to my livin' quarters, and we'll have us a sure 'nuff reunion.'

'Plenty of time to catch up, son.' The old man reached out to pat his old friend upon the shoulder before turning to stride from the hardware shop. 'Plenty of time to catch up.' His repeated the words to himself as he stepped from the doorway to pace toward the patient charcoal tied to the hitching post out front.

After delivering Jimmy to the local livery, Russell made the decision to treat himself to a genuine luxury. Stopping in at the hotel, the only freshly painted building in town, he asked for a room complete with feather bed and a tub.

'I aim to take me a steaming hot, all-over bath!' The scout pulled soiled fingers through the dirty, grey beard as he announced his intentions to the delicate, scented clerk with the well-oiled hair. 'Then I'm gonna sleep an hour or so in that big, clean fluffy bed.'

'Certainly, sir,' the little clerk spoke through his nose with a sneer. His manner implied that his customer might be in sore need of the tub and water. 'I'll have the boy bring up plenty of soap as well, Mr Russell.'

'You do that, Prissy.' Three Toes cackled with delight in the young man's arrogance while he plucked the brass key from the polished mahogany counter. He turned to cross the small, carpeted lobby to the narrow stairway. 'Jist tell that boy to hurry up with that hot bath water. I ain't a man to be kept waitin'!' The old man trudged up the stairs with his bedroll and Henry repeater in hand.

A short time later, he sat in the hot, soapy water with a mist of steam hovering about his neck and head. As he soaked his tired body in the warm, soothing water, Russell considered the hardware store man and their long association. A grin twisted his whisk-ered lips at the alias his old companion had chosen. Joshua Easterly was, in fact, famed gunman Elijah West. According to news-paper reports, West had been killed in a gun battle up in the Montana Territory a few years back. Obviously, the reports were false, but Russell was curious to hear the story that went along with his friend's mysterious disappearance into this anonymous exist-ence in the little village of Spit Junction.

Three Toes had first worked with Elijah West when they served together in the Mexican War. At that time, the young man had only been on the far western frontier for a few short years, but had already become a hardened Westerner and a fine hand with the weapons he carried. From Mexico, the two men had drifted north for a few years of trapping in the Rockies and then had done a stint or two scouting for the army. After parting company, Russell had stayed close to the mountains while West drifted off to engage in a mixed variety of occupations including cowboy, lawman, and, eventually, gunman. The two old friends had stayed in touch over the years, but had not seen one another since that summer of 1878 when West had dropped from sight after his supposedly fatal Montana shootout. Now, in the spring of 1881, the two were reunited once more upon the high plains of the Texas Panhandle. The old man's head began to nod as he relaxed in the comforting tub of water. His thoughts scattered and drifted to dreams then back again as his eyes opened with a start. 'A nap in that soft bed is what I need.' Once again the grin twisted his whiskered lips while his grey head nodded. 'A short nap then off to the Emerald Palace Saloon.' The trapper rose from the tub to spend an hour in that soft, feather bed.

The Emerald Palace Saloon was a shabby barroom with faded green paint spread in a thin coat over plank walls. A dozen scarred, round tables were scattered about the room. Sawdust covered the floor. Little had been done by way of decoration with only an occasional advertising poster breaking the monotony of washed-out emerald green. A wooden bar ran the length of the room and behind it stood the saloon's proud owner, Gerry O'Cooners.

'Step up, step up, first drink is on the house, me friend!' The big Irishman grinned from ear to ear as he welcomed the arrival of the grizzled old mountain man. Orange-red hair topped a freckled face with a prominent broken nose. The features had shamrock written across them while the six foot frame and scarred knuckles screamed 'boxer'. Gerry O'Cooners towered above William Russell as the trapper approached the bar. 'Welcome to me establishment.'

'Thank you, kindly,' Three Toes grinned as

he reached for the small shot of whiskey the big Irishman had placed on the counter before him. Taking the glass in hand, he quickly surveyed the room to find some dozen or so assorted cowboys, all engaged in good natured conversation and card games. The scout raised the glass to his lips and belted down the drink. The cheap rotgut stung his throat and brought tears to his eyes. From there, it burned a path to his belly where it seemed to eat a hole clean through to his buckskins.

'Damn, but that's good,' he managed to croak out through lips twisted in a tight grimace. 'I'll have another.'

Russell and the red-headed giant fell into a friendly banter that rambled on for a full half hour before anyone else entered through the sagging batwing doors of the small saloon. Finally, the Irishman's face brightened as the doors parted to allow new customers entrance. Russell turned his head to examine the new arrivals, but let out a groan as his green eyes fell upon the familiar couple.

'I'll be daglasted!' Russell grumbled.

'Greetings!' The two Easterners chorused their salutation. Professors Milton T. Robertson and Tillery J. Montgomery crossed the sawdust-covered floor to stand before the bar next to the freshly scrubbed trapper. Broad grins enlivened their features. Each seemed delighted to have found the man who had assisted them along the trail.

'My, my, but we have looked high and low for you since our arrival in this lovely little community, Mr Russell,' Robertson began.

'Indeed,' Montgomery added, 'I believe we have a valuable proposition for you.'

O'Cooners stood with his jaw hanging slack for a moment before collecting his wits about him and mumbling something about the first drink being on the house. Splashing the amber liquid into two chipped glasses, the big Irishman stared at the eastern college professors with open amazement. They might as well have been Chinese royalty, so foreign were their manners, speech, and appearance.

Without hesitation, the two professors politely raised the small glasses in toast to Three Toes. Smiles widened from ear to ear as they lifted glasses in salute.

'To our benefactor,' Robertson spoke with good cheer.

'Hear, hear!' agreed Montgomery.

Russell looked on in amusement. He nodded his head in acceptance of the toast while waiting for the Easterners to get a taste of the harsh whiskey sloshing about in the little glasses they held before them. He grinned in anticipation of their reaction to the burning, amber liquor.

As one, the two professors belted back the rotgut whiskey, then quickly pulled handkerchiefs from their jacket pockets to blot daintily at their lips. Neither blinked an eye nor choked back a cough. Instead, each grinned broadly before offering up compliments to the barkeep.

'We'll have another, please,' the two spoke in unison in even, steady tones.

'I'll be sheep dipped!' Russell exclaimed,

but the Easterners only looked on with puzzled expressions.

'Mr Russell,' Robertson spoke with conviction, 'my colleague and I feel that you are the man we can trust to lead us forward upon our expedition.'

'I ain't interested.' Three Toes returned to the drink he was nursing along before him on the scarred counter top.

'Oh, really, Mr Russell,' Montgomery joined the conversation, 'we really do require your services. You see, we have a map drawn up by an earlier expedition. We do believe that a man of your abilities could take us right to the find of the century. A wealth of scientific treasure awaits us some-where here in this very region!'

'No.'

'But we do have a map…'

'No.'

'We could make a remarkable discovery together…'

'No.'

'We'll reward you handsomely…'

'No.'

'We'll...'

'No!' Russell's tone was firm, but he attempted to temper his refusal with some advice. 'Boys, I got to be movin' on north. I've got a home up in the mountains of Montana and I aim to spend the fall and winter up there. I'm sorry, but I jist ain't got the time to be runnin' around with you fellers alookin' fer some dang fool scientific treasure. Ask around,' the old man continued, 'you'll find somebody what can show you the lay of the land.'

'Certainly, Mr Russell,' Robertson nodded his head in congenial agreement.

'Indeed,' Montgomery grinned as the two stepped away from the bar to mingle throughout the smoke-filled room.

The pair of professors began to make the rounds of tables scattered about the room asking each man present if he could show them about the region. Meanwhile, Russell resumed sipping his whiskey and bantering about with the red-head behind the bar. It took less than five minutes for the trouble to begin.

'Excuse us, please.' Three Toes heard Robertson's ever pleasant tones over the general noise of the room.

'Yes, do pardon us, please,' Montgomery added his own voice to that of his partner's.

'Oh we'll pardon and excuse you gents all to hell and back!' the reply boomed through the small barroom as the old trapper groaned again. Without even turning around, he knew what he would find. He also knew that it would be necessary to bail the two college teachers out of another messy situation.

'What'll I do, Lenny?'

Three Toes turned to see a cowboy hovering above the professors. The man stood close to seven feet tall and upon that large frame carried some three hundred pounds. Dressed in typical range gear, the man was probably in his mid-twenties, and was taking his direction from the slick, thirty-something cowpoke who remained seated at the table with two other range riding companions.

'I think you need to show them dudes how to behave themselves,' Lenny, the slick cowboy, spoke softly. Russell noted that the little man kept his hand close to the Colt .45 holstered high on his right hip. The other two cowpokes looked on with amusement animating their scruffy features.

'If you don't mind, sir.' Robertson smiled at the big man who held his shirt front crumpled in a huge left fist.

'Indeed, sir, if you'll excuse us, please.' Montgomery looked down at the same man's right fist holding his own shirt front in a tight grip.

'You interrupted our game, mister.' Lenny's tone was flat. 'I had a good hand when you stumbled in here with your questions. I think that Hank here needs to teach you gents a few western manners.'

'I can do it, Lenny.' Hank's whisker-stubbled face split into a wide grin. 'I can hit 'em both real hard!'

'Really, sir, we meant no harm…'

'I'm not interested in what you meant,'

Lenny snarled. 'When you poke your fancy manners into my poker game, then I'm gonna have Hank here take a little satisfaction outa your big city hides.'

Three Toes let his gaze shift from Lenny to Hank as he heard the big man growl deep in his throat. Obviously, big Hank was a few cards shy of a full deck, and little Lenny called all the shots. Nevertheless, it was Hank who held Robertson and Montgomery firmly in his grasp, so it was the giant that the old trapper knew he must deal with first.

Taking the scene in at a glance, Russell made the decision to plunge head first into the trouble that confronted him. In his thinking, there was no turning back now. These four hardcase cowboys were not bandits nor outlaws, but only troublesome cowhands out for a night on the town. They had picked the wrong time and place for their shenanigans. The buckskin-clad scout hoped he did not have to kill them before the evening came to an end, but that would depend on Lenny and his companions.

'Go ahead, Hank.' Lenny's lips twitched in a slight smile as he instructed his large companion to begin the assault upon his cheerfully passive victims.

'First up, I'm gonna pound you.' Hank looked down at the two men he held tightly in his strong grip. His slow brain could not understand why neither man appeared frightened or even disturbed by the turn of events. 'Then, I might just cut you a bit before I...'

'I'd be willin' to bet that I'd provide you boys with a good deal more sport fer the evenin',' Three Toes spoke up in a sharp, challenging tone as he interrupted the slow-witted behemoth standing across the floor of the saloon.

'Mind your own business, old man,' Lenny spoke warily from his position at the table. 'We don't want any trouble with you.'

'Now, I'm right pleased to hear that,' Russell gave his words a sarcastic twist, 'but you already got trouble with me you no 'count saddle trash. Tell your gorilly there to take his hands off a them two dudes and sit his big butt back down at the table. We've heard enough outa both of you to last us fer the entire night.'

Astonishment washed over Lenny's features while Hank simply looked on in bewildered silence. Slowly, the big fingers lost their grip upon the shirt fronts. The professors quickly struggled free of the giant's grasping paws before scurrying across the floor to join Russell at the bar. From this vantage point, they watched events unfold without any indication of concern.

'You got quite a mouth on you for such an old man.' Lenny narrowed his eyes, but kept his tone soft as he measured the mountain man who now stood with his back to the long counter.

'And you got a smart mouth fer sich a young pup,' Russell grinned. 'Besides which, your friend here has an ugly face. Now, you boys gonna go on with your card game, or do I have to come over there to kick some sense into your thick skulls?'

'Don't bite off more'n you can chew old-timer.' Lenny wanted out of the deadly exchange but struggled to save face. 'We were just teasin' with them gents anyhow. No call for you and me to tangle over a couple of dudes.'

'No call exceptin' I'm jist cantankerous enough to take some pleasure out of a wool-ley ruckus with a pack of young bucks sich as you boys.' Three Toes took a few steps forward. 'Now, what's it gonna be boys? Play the hand you dealt or keep your damn mouths shut!'

'No reason for all this...' Lenny began again.

Russell took another step toward the table.

'Lenny?' Hank's puzzled expression looked for some clue as to his next course of action.

'Take the crazy old coot, Hank.' Lenny's voice betrayed his apprehension. 'Teach the old mountain goat a few manners.'

'You jist do that, sonny.' Three Toes seemed to glide across the room in a flash. A moccasined foot caught the big man between the legs while claw-like hands reached out to grab handfuls of stringy brown hair. Pulling the head down and bringing his knee up, Russell felt the man's nose fragment before he let the giant drop to the sawdust covered floor. Crimson spurting from the broken nose, Hank moaned in pain from both the broken nose and his tender groin. His saddle partners quickly scrambled to their feet with Lenny in the lead.

'That's gonna cost you…' Lenny spoke up in harsh tones but found his words intersrupted by a hard, knobby fist that sent three teeth flying loose into his mouth. Scarlet dripped from his chin as the little cowboy spat out two teeth while swallowing the third.

The other two men stepped back for a moment as Three Toes grinned in triumph. Quickly, the old man's good humour faded as he felt powerful arms wrap around his wiry frame. Arms clamped tightly to his sides, Russell knew he was in for a beating. Hank had risen silently to his feet to approach from the rear.

'I done good, huh, Lenny?' Hank's grin looked sick through the flood of crimson that ran from his broken nose.

'You done fine, Hank.' Lenny's missing teeth gave the cowboy a slight lisp. 'It's time to learn your manners now, Pappy.' He spoke with a snarl that bought only a sneer from the trapper.

'Go to hell you bastard!' Russell spit right in the cowboy's face.

'By damn, I'll…' Lenny advanced with his right fist knotted tightly.

'Let him go.'

Everything stopped in the small barroom. The voice carried a note of command that the slow-witted Hank immediately obeyed. Russell struggled free from the giant's embrace to make his way to the bar while everyone turned their attention to the new-comer standing just inside the batwing doors.

'That's fine boys.' Joshua Easterly offered up a smile that never travelled as far as the hard, sky-blue eyes which seemed cold as ice. 'No harm done. Just move along real easy like and we'll all call it a night.'

'What is this?' Lenny recovered from the sudden arrival of Easterly. 'An old folks reunion?'

'Somethin' like that,' Easterly spoke with his familiar easy grin. 'No cause in you folks gettin' all hot and bothered over a used up old man like that.' He indicated Three Toes now standing at the bar nursing a new shot of rotgut supplied by the ever-ready O'Cooners. 'Anybody can see he ain't worth the time and effort.'

The trapper muttered something under his breath, but let his old friend have sport with him. The least he could do was to let old Elijah West handle this the way he saw fit.

'He owes us for some pain!' Lenny growled.

'Just call it even and move along, son.' Easterly spoke softly. 'Let it end before someone else gets hurt.'

'I'll be damned if I'll let some old...' Lenny exploded into action. His right hand darted for the Colt .45 at his right hip, and the gun cleared leather with surprising speed. The other three looked on in startled fascination at this deadly turn of events.

BOOM! BOOM!

Two shots sounded from the Colt Navy .36. Crimson gushed from the chest of Lenny as the little cowboy slammed against the wall. The Colt .45 fell from the man's grip as he slumped to a sitting position in the sawdust before falling forward in a heap. Joshua Easterly, hardware store owner, stood silently, grimly, with eyes fixed upon the remaining three cowhands.

'I had no choice, boys.' He shook his silver head in resignation. 'Now, take him on out and all of you ride on clear of town.'

Without another word the three men did as they were told. The cowboys wanted no more trouble tonight. A little fun had already gone much too far.

'That was a lucky shot, Mr Easterly.' Gerry O'Cooners spoke up quickly as soon as the men left.

'Somehow luck ain't what I had in mind,'

the gunman spoke softly with a touch of sadness. Quickly, he ordered a bottle of the best Tennessee whiskey and left Russell, Robertson, Montgomery, and O'Cooners standing in silence. After a few mumbled exchanges, the two Easterners decided to call it a night and promised to look up Three Toes in the morning. After they left the room and the remaining customers settled back to their conversation, Russell turned his attention to the big Irishman behind the bar.

'You know who he is, don't you?' the trapper asked.

'I know he's Elijah West, if that's what you be askin'.' The freckled face broke into a grin. 'I've known ever since he arrived here almost three years ago.'

'Why haven't you said anything?' Three Toes offered up a puzzled expression. 'Why haven't you told anyone?'

'Sure and now, I figure Mr Easterly must have good cause to want to leave Elijah West behind him. I see no reason to deny him his peace.'

'You're a good man, Irish!' The scout reached out to pat the red-head upon his arm. 'You've a good head and kind heart; there's no finer combination.'

William Russell nursed his whiskey in silence. He would give Elijah West a few minutes to settle his nerves before slipping around to the back door of the hardware shop. He would wait a few more minutes. A grin twisted his whiskered lips once more. Tonight was a night for good whiskey and good friends; both brought a warm feeling to the old man's insides.

FOUR

The room behind the hardware store was small; no more than twelve by fifteen feet. Clean, plank floors were covered by an occasional rag rug. The few rectangular rugs and the patchwork quilt covering the narrow bed brought the room some measure of colour. Other than the bed shoved against a drab wall, the room's only furnishings consisted of a tiny, round table, a two drawer-double door washstand with bowl and pitcher, a large wooden chest that rested at the foot of the bed, and a sturdy bookcase filled with miscellaneous leather bound volumes ranging from Shakespeare to Cooper. Two ladder-back chairs sat at the little oak table. An oil lamp burned low to illuminate the tiny room. The walls were bare except for an advertising calendar tacked to the wall just inside the back door. Elijah West and William Russell sat across from one another with the half-empty bottle of whiskey upon the table between them. Each man slowly sipped the amber nectar with obvious delight; each understood the value of good friends as well as good Tennessee whiskey.

'Shaved off the moustache,' Three Toes commented idly as he wiped his mouth with the back of his hand. The old man's meadow-green eyes seemed to twinkle in the lamp light as he examined the features of his long-time friend.

'Yeah,' the man now known as Joshua Easterly nodded in agreement. 'Shaved off the lip hair and gave up my bandana, jacket, and left-hand pistol.' The hardware store owner referred to the blue bandana he had habitually worn along with the fringed buckskin jacket. In the 'old' days of Elijah West, he had always carried a matching set of Colt Navy .36 revolvers, modified from the old cap and ball, now the mate to the one on his right hip rested in the big chest at the foot of the bed. 'I ain't used that left hand pistol in quite a spell anyway,' West concluded. 'Not since busting my hand up yonder in the Montana Territory a few years back.'

'I do recall,' the old scout spoke softly as he remembered fondly their last visit together in the rugged mountains of western Montana. 'I seen your jacket on the back of a young sprout down in south east Texas recently. That's still some handsome coat even after all these many years of wear.'

'Yeah,' West's smile was almost lost in the dim light of the small room, 'I give it to young Wheeler McKay of the Bar W spread to wear in good health. Maybe it'll keep the chill off him for a few years to come.' Silence gripped the room for a few minutes as the friends lifted tumblers to their lips to sip at the fine whiskey. They had spent the past few hours drinking, talking, and catching up with one another's lives. 'You know, it is amazing what a few simple changes and a tricky news story can do for a man.'

A few years back, Elijah West had been involved in a showdown in the small town of Big Rock, Montana. The editor of the local newspaper, sympathetic to the plight of the aging gunfighter, had manufactured a story in which West had been killed in a blazing Montana shootout. This news item had been picked up by wire services all over the country, so old enemies, and old friends alike, now assumed the gunman to be dead. Since that time, West had drifted south to visit with his old friend Bullwhip Wallace at the Bar W Ranch in south east Texas, where he had left his jacket with the youngster, Wheeler McKay, and then he had come north to settle in the Texas Panhandle. With a few minor changes in dress, giving up the second pistol, and shaving the silver moustache, West had successfully passed himself off as Joshua Easterly these past few years. He now led the peaceful, comfortable life of a shop keeper in the small town of Spit Junction, Texas.

'That barkeep, O'Cooners,' Russell paused as he licked precious drops from his lips, 'he knows who you are, son.'

'I suspected as much,' West replied. 'He covered for me tonight with that talk of a lucky shot. He knows,' the gunman nodded soberly, 'but he won't say anything. Gerry's a good man, he can keep his mouth shut.'

'I'd agree with you on that one,' the mountain man grinned in the dim light as he shifted the conversation to another subject. 'You know, Elijah, it looks to me like you got yourself an admirer, boy.'

'What're you talkin' about old man?'

'Hell, you know what I'm talkin' about,' the old trapper cackled with laughter. 'Don't be playin' dumb with this old coon. I'm talkin' about that purty thang that was in your store this afternoon when I hit town.'

'That's the widder school marm.' West's face flushed crimson while he stumbled for words. 'Betty Shafer's a looker all right, but she ain't interested in a broken down old man such as me.'

'She seemed right interested to me, son.' Russell spoke in earnest now, all hint of teasing gone from his voice. 'You jist needs to screw up your courage and let the lady know how you feel about her. No point in living out your days alone when there's a soft, purty lady willin' to provide you companionship. There's times when I wish that...' The old mountain man shook his head sadly, but never completed the sentence. Instead he gulped down a swallow of whiskey while staring at the scarred table top before him.

'You gonna help out them college fellers

or not?' The silver-haired gunman spoke up quickly to shift the direction of the conversation once again. Earlier in the evening, Russell had told of his meeting with the two men and their plans for some sort of scientific expedition in the Panhandle region. 'Sounds to me like an easy job,' he sipped the whiskey, 'and you could use the work to pick up a few dollars to see you through the winter.'

'There's sure 'nuff somethin' to be said fer that.' Three Toes pondered the situation carefully before continuing, 'But they's a strange pair and besides, if I don't git myself back home to the mountains purty soon, then I'll be stuck down here for the winter without no place to stay. I ain't spent too many winters away from home, and I'm lookin' to move along.'

'You could stay here.' The gunman spoke softly, but let his sky-blue eyes fasten upon his friend's leathery features. 'I don't see how it could do any harm. No one's likely to connect us if we play it right.'

'I ain't never stayed in no town fer so long a stretch,' the trapper shook his grey head in careful deliberation, 'but I'll admit to you that them cold mountain winters can really deal these old bones a fit.'

'Then do the job for the professors.' West's smile was warm and inviting. 'Show them birds around the Panhandle, then stay in town with me for the cold season.' The gun-man knew now that his friend would agree to stay on through the fall and winter months. He would work for the Easterners into the summer then make his home in Spit Junction before cold weather came to the high plains. 'I could use an old man like you to help out around here. Maybe I'll let you sweep the floors or clean out the little house out back.'

'Huh,' the old man snorted in derision, 'and jist maybe I'll help you git up enough courage to ask out that widder woman you're so took with, but too old and too stubborn to admit it. One of us is an old fool, son,' Russell winked at his friend as he lifted his glass in a toast, 'and it ain't me.'

West's face turned scarlet once more as he returned the toast before draining the Tennessee whiskey from his glass. Replacing the tumbler upon the battered oak table before him, the gunman stretched out muscled arms and yawned.

'Time for me to call it a night,' he announced.

'Same here.' Three Toes rose to his feet while pushing back his chair from the table. 'I got a soft bed waiting fer me over to the hotel. I'll be up early to connect with them Easterners. Soon as I lay in a few supplies, I'll get Milly and Tilly outa town lookin' fer them dagblasted old bones of theirs. You take care and I'll be seein' you when we git back to town.'

'Good night, old man,' West winked at the wiry figure that opened the door to step into the darkened back alleyway. 'Take care of yourself.'

'Night to you too and old man yourself,' Russell called over his shoulder as he shut the door. Retreating into the darkness, the mountain man mumbled to himself, 'I been takin' care of myself fer nigh onto seventy years now, and suppose I can look out fer a couple of high falootin' college professors as well.' He continued to mutter and grumble as he made his way back to the hotel and soft bed that awaited him there. After a good night's sleep, the old man would be back on the trail again.

'This here map takes us right into Palo Duro Canyon,' William Russell spoke to the men who sat their horses to the rear of his big, black stallion. 'I ain't been through that big ditch in nigh onto twenty years. From what I can see here, it looks like we got to git right down onto the canyon floor.'

'My goodness but that does sound exciting.' Professor Milton T. Robertson's small frame perched upon the little pony with precarious balance. His slight figure was dressed as usual in canvas pants, knee boots, and brown shirt. The pith helmet saved his bald pate from the sun, but the hawk nose and large ears stuck out from beneath the shade of the wide brim. 'We shall be thrilled to examine the colourful canyon walls. Is that not correct my dear, fellow?'

'Absolutely, my fine friend,' Professor Tillery J. Montgomery nodded his freckled head in agreement. Bright red hair stuck out from under his own pith helmet and his large stocky frame was dressed the same as his companion. The thick glasses made his eyes appear twice their normal size while his usual ear to ear smile animated his wholesome features. Shifting his weight about uncomfortably, it was obvious that the man was uneasy in the saddle. 'We have heard many wonderful stories of the colour and beauty of Palo Duro Canyon. No doubt, this will prove to be an exhilarating experience.'

'No doubt,' Russell mimicked the Easterner's tone as he folded up the map and stuffed it into his open shirt front. The old scout was dressed in the only clothing he owned. The old, stained buckskins and moccasins had served him for many seasons. At his right hip rested the Smith and Wesson American .44 and at his left sat the big Bowie. A tomahawk protruded from his belt while the big Henry rifle rested across his thighs. The ragged fur cap upon his head seemed almost to blend with the long, grey whiskers that covered his face. Only the bright, green eyes hinted at the quick wit and good humour the mountain man was known for among his friends. 'What you fellers don't seem to understand is that gettin' down in that canyon ain't no easy chore,' the trapper commented as he scratched at his whiskers with claw-like fingers, 'and gettin' out again ain't much better.'

'Oh, we'll be fine, Mr Russell,' Robertson assured the guide with good cheer, 'you can depend on us.'

'To be certain, Mr Russell,' Montgomery agreed with us usual grin in place, 'we're of sturdy New England stock.'

'I hope so.' Russell sobered as he turned the conversation to the task ahead. 'Now, you fellers fill me in jist one more time on what this here thing is all about, will you?'

'Certainly!' Robertson responded with enthusiasm. 'Several years ago a dear colleague of ours came west in search of signs of prehistoric life; fossilized dinosaur bones to be more specific. He was most interested in locating the remains of ancient mastodon that roamed this territory thousands of years ago...'

'Mastawhats?' Russell queried. The old man was already confused by the story the two professors had told over and over since they left Spit Junction early in the new day. Now, some ten miles out of town, they had paused to rest the horses and examine the map.

'Mastodons,' Mongtomery answered and then picked up the story. 'Our colleague located a likely site upon the floor of the Palo Duro Canyon. He had neither the time nor the funds to continue his expedition and has since turned the project over to us.'

'Jist what is one these here mastodons?'

Russell asked of the professors seated to his rear.

'They were giant, woolly, elephant-like beasts that lived in this region many thousands of years ago,' Montgomery answered.

'So, what is it that you want with some hairy elephink bones?' the scout asked with genuine curiosity. 'I mean, even if we find the critter's bones, jist what good is they goin' to do you? What're them things worth?'

'Why, they're priceless!' Robertson squealed in his excitement.

'Why, they're beyond value!' Montgomery almost shouted in his joy.

'You mean they's worthless.' Russell scowled before adding. 'You gents better have the cash on hand to pay me when this job is done. I ain't got no use fer no elephink bones and that's a dagblasted fact!'

'I can assure you that will be paid in cash, Mr Russell.' Robertson held his helmet in one hand as he wiped a hand across his hairless dome. A sly grin spread across his bird-like features. 'You'll be paid whether or not we find the bones we seek.'

'However,' Professor Montgomery used a handkerchief to clean his thick spectacles as he spoke, 'should we find the fossils, there will be a five hundred dollar bonus added to the promised fee.'

'What's that you say, sonny?' The old mountain man twisted his wiry frame about in the saddle and squinted hard at the two grinning professors who sat their ponies a short distance behind him. 'You two pullin' my leg?'

'No sir, Mr Russell,' Robertson assured him, 'if we find what we are seeking, then you shall have a five hundred dollar bonus to reward your efforts.'

'I would dare say that this tidy sum should see you through a warm, safe winter,' Montgomery observed.

'I'd dare say it myself, gents.' Russell's wrinkled leathery features broke into a broad smile. 'You'd best git your purses out, fer if there's bones to be found then we're a gonna find 'em. Let's ride!' Three Toes touched heels to Jimmy. The black stallion took off like a shot, leaving the professor in a cloud of choking dust.

'I heard it all, Bill.' Len Holt and the outlaw boss sat around an upturned packing crate that served as a table in the dirty, littered room. 'There's two prissy dudes in town talkin' with an old fur trapper about the treasure. They got a map and everything.'

'I'll be damned!' Bad Eye Bill Malone licked a few remaining drops of whiskey from his lips. Already, even at this early hour of the day, he was well on his way to being drunk. He rubbed dirty, stubby fingers over the bristles upon his chin. 'All this searchin' fer that money when some eastern pretty boys has got a map that will take us right to the gold! Looks to me like our troubles is over, Len. Tell it all to me again.'

The diminutive gunman recounted the story of the night before. He had been seated in the dim corner of the Emerald Palace Saloon when he had overheard minor bits and pieces of the conversation between the mountain man and the eastern college professors. The parts he had understood clearly were 'map' and 'treasure', so Holt was now convinced that the oddly matched trio were on the trail of the lost federal payroll being hunted by the Malone gang. After a restless night in town, the little shootist had hurried to the camp in a washed out gully some few miles from town. Malone had his headquarters in a small weathered shack furnished with assorted primitive pieces while the remainder of the men camped beneath the stars nearby. As Holt related the events of the previous evening, he was interrupted by the one-eyed bandit leader who squinted at the little gunman with his one good hazel eye.

'Just who in the hell was the old gun toter who saved the mountain goat's hide?' Malone growled his question before gulping another shot of rotgut whiskey.

'I don't know.' Len Holt grew quiet. 'He just came out of nowhere to shoot up the cowhand who fancied himself a gunfighter, then he bought himself a bottle of whiskey and left.'

Malone's bloodshot eye showed contempt. 'Just some no account townie with a lucky shot...'

'No.' Holt's tone was firm; firm with a note of caution that hinted at trouble.

'What do you mean?' Malone snorted his arrogant response. 'So he put some lead in a two-bit cowpuncher. That don't make him Wyatt Earp.'

'He's not to be taken for granted.' The little gunman's tone was grim. 'He was fast and,' Holt let his eyes lock upon the red, watery orb of Malone, 'more important, he was accurate.'

'Faster than you Len?' Malone asked his long-time companion the question while he casually filled the chipped, dirty tumbler with whiskey. 'Could he take you in a fair fight?'

'I didn't say that!' The gunfighter exploded in anger as he slammed a fist down upon the rough wood of the packing crate between them. 'There ain't nobody that can beat me to the draw.' He visibly took control of his temper, then spoke in a more steady tone. 'I just mean that we ought to steer clear of the old man. There ain't no point in lookin' for trouble when we're on the edge of the biggest take in our whole lives.'

'That's a right good point, partner,' Malone's reassuring tone served to soothe the other man's hurt pride. 'No reason for you to shoot it out with some old hellion in a no account town like Spit Junction. Hell, we'll stop over for supplies then be on the trail of those three with the map.' He grinned a foul looking display of greed and evil intent. 'We'll find us the treasure and then get rid of the witnesses. The world won't miss one old man and a couple of eastern dudes.'

'You're the boss, Bill.' Len Holt slipped the pistol from his right hand holster in order to feel the comforting weight of the .45 in his hand. 'You're the boss.'

'Damn right!' Bill Malone rose to his feet knocking over the crude stool that had supported his bulk. He crossed the littered floor to kick open the plank door that hung loosely upon rusted hinges. 'Mount up, boys! Get ready to ride for Spit Junction within the half hour.'

FIVE

The two professors had spent a quiet night beneath the stars with the leather-tough old mountain man. He had awakened the pair before first light to the aroma of boiling coffee, sizzling bacon, and simmering beans. They watched darkness melt to pink along the horizon as they finished a final cup of the thick, black brew while Russell readied the animals for the day's travel. The spring day retained some of winter's chill, but all knew that the sun would soon warm the flat, wind-swept plains. Daybreak in the Texas Panhandle left the Easterners in awe of the rugged beauty that surrounded them on all sides.

'We ought to hit the Palo Duro by early this afternoon,' Russell called over his shoulder as he saddled Jimmy. The big, black nickered at the sound of his master's voice. 'We'll probably camp along the rim afore headin' on down first thing in the mornin'.'

'Anything you say, Mr Russell,' Professor Robertson spoke up in cheery good humour. He sipped from the big, tin mug with obvious pleasure. 'We will, of course, follow your every lead.'

'Certainly, sir,' Professor Montgomery assured their guide, 'we are so pleased you decided to accompany us that you can depend upon our complete cooperation.'

'Horsefeathers!' grumbled the trapper as he tightened the charcoal's cinch strap a final hitch. 'Put them cups up and git on your horses. We got miles to put behind us and the day ain't gettin' any younger while we sit jawin'.'

The morning passed without incident. The

flat, almost treeless plains seemed to stretch endlessly beyond the horizon. Scrubby brush and sage scattered across the landscape with an occasional eruption of stone to interrupt the otherwise level terrain. Slow, steady progress had been made while the sun climbed high into the sky. Throughout the morning, Robertson and Montgomery carried on an endless commentary upon their surroundings while Russell did his best to ignore his eastern charges.

'I simply can not express my delight in this lovely country,' Professor Robertson observed to his companion. 'Really, this region is among the most impressive I have ever encountered.'

'No doubt about it my dear, Professor,' Montgomery agreed. 'The beauty of this Texas Panhandle is unsurpassed in our many years of travel.'

'Quite so,' Robertson nodded his head. 'Why I actually do believe that...'

'Hold up!' Russell called out as he reined in Jimmy. 'Let's pull up over in the shade of them boulders fer a little noon-time snack while we rest the horses fer a spell. It's about time we...'

BOOM!

One shot rang out that shattered the still, quiet air of the high plains. The professors looked on in horror as their guide pitched from his saddle to sprawl face-first into the hard, rocky earth beside his horse. Jimmy, startled by the shot, pranced away from the area to wait some fifty yards from his master's fallen form. Robertson and Montgomery sat in shocked, still silence.

'Don't nobody move!' Bad Eye Bill Malone shouted in a voice that resembled the roar of a wounded bear. No one moved as the outlaw leader stepped from the safety of the cluster of boulders beside the trail. Close on his heels followed the three hardcase owlhoots that comprised Malone's ruthless gang. All had guns drawn to point in the general direction of the professors while the boss outlaw's Remington Frontier .44 remained fixed upon the motionless form of the buckskin clad mountain man. 'Come on down, Len! You got the only one with any gumption.'

Professsors Robertson and Montgomery looked on in silence as the little gunman climbed down from his hiding place. Holt had been waiting high in the jumbled mound of boulders that sat beside the trail leading north from Spit Junction to Palo Duro Canyon. In addition to the holstered twin Colt .45 revolvers, the gunfighter now carried a Winchester rifle in his hands. His face wore a smirk of satisfaction. He joined his boss while keeping the muzzle of his weapon in line with the old man's sprawled figure. Together, the two badmen approached Holt's target with caution.

'Keep your eyes on 'im, Len,' Malone warned his right hand man as he holstered his own pistol and knelt before the prone form that lay upon the rugged plains. Reaching out a rough, calloused paw, the big outlaw jerked Russell over upon his back. A nasty wound across the scout's scalp flowed crimson while scarlet leaked from his battered nose. A pool of blood had already soaked the earth beneath the trapper's head so his hair stuck to the ground in a sticky, tangled mass. Russell's irregular breathing rasped through his open mouth in shallow gasps.

'He ain't dead,' Malone growled, 'but he won't last long out here on the Staked Plains. His head is busted open and there's enough blood here to have dropped a buffalo.'

'Want me to make sure?' Len Holt smiled as he worked the lever of the Winchester in anticipation. 'One more bullet would do the job.'

'Naw,' the outlaw boss grinned as his hazel eye shifted to the little gunman. 'What do we care whether or not the old goat lives or dies? It don't make me no nevermind.' Letting his gaze drift to the two wide-eyed figures seated in a grim silence upon their mounts, the one-eyed badman shouted a query in fierce tones. 'Where the hell's that map?'

'Pardon me?' Robertson's expression

changed from shock to confusion as he pondered the outlaw's question.

'The map?' Holt interjected.

'Excuse me?' Montgomery shook his head as he struggled to understand what the bandits wanted from them.

'You know damn well what we're lookin' for, so don't get funny with us, you green-horned idjits,' Malone growled out his anger. 'We're lookin' for that treasure map that you two've been braggin' about and we aim to have it!'

'The only map we have is in the possession of Mr Russell,' Robertson said as he let his eyes drift back to the bloody form that stretched upon the rocky earth.

'I believe he placed the document inside his shirt front,' Montgomery added. 'However, I really cannot see how our map would be of any interest to...'

'You two just shut up and keep still,' the outlaw chief commanded as he stuffed a rough hand into Russell's buckskin shirt. A moment later the big man removed his dirty paw tightly clutching the map. 'Bring up the horses! Let's mount up and ride boys. This trail ain't travelled a heap, but we don't need to be here when somebody comes across this old man's mangy carcass. Let the stink birds and coyotes have their fill. We're headed for Palo Duro Canyon.'

'Why, surely you don't mean to leave poor Mr Russell here without...' Robertson's voice sounded sharply in the tension filled atmosphere. A look from Malone silenced him. The outlaw's hazel eye conveyed deadly menace as he glared at the Easterner with unconcealed hatred. However, Montgomery could not contain his frustration.

'I really must protest this outrage!' The freckled face turned red beneath the pith helmet.

'You'll both keep your mouths shut!' Malone exploded in a fit of rage. 'I got the map now and I'll have the treasure we been lookin' fer afore the week is out. You two city dudes is comin' along with us until we find the stash. I can tell this here map takes us up to the canyon, but I can't make out these scribbles and scrabbles on this here paper. We might need you prissy boys to help out.' The big bandit's voice began a threatening promise. 'I ain't gonna kill you right now cause I might need you,' his eye squinted as he shifted the hazel orb from face to face, 'but if you give me any trouble, I'll hurt you bad. That's a fact!'

The professors sat in silence again as the three hardcases brought the horses from their hiding place in the rocks beside the trail. Malone and Holt mounted their horses to take the lead while Robertson and Montgomery followed close behind with the remaining three outlaws bringing up the rear. Pushing their mounts hard, they left the grisly scene behind them. A half-hearted effort at catching Jimmy had proven unsuccessful, so the big stallion remained behind to stand quietly beside the trapper who stretched upon his back in the noon sun. The patch of earth beneath the old man's head had already turned black and sticky as the death birds began to gather overhead.

His head seemed to burst in pain with each beat of his heart. Consciousness returned slowly to the strong-willed mountain man. As he regained his senses, he felt warmth from a nearby fire and, upon opening his eyes, realized that night had fallen. The cool, crisp air of the spring night did not penetrate the old man's bones due to the pleasant blaze of the camp fire and the thick, wool blanket covering his lanky form. His bandaged head rested easily upon another blanket what had been rolled to form a crude pillow. Other than his pounding head, the trapper felt good.

'About time you come to, old man,' a gentle voice spoke from across the fire. 'I always knew that hard head of yours could stop lead, but now you've proved it for sure.'

Russell could make out the figure of Elijah West seated close to the fire. In spite of the throbbing pain inside his head, the old man managed a reassuring grin for his old companion.

'Jist hush and git me a cup of that witch's brew you call coffee,' Russell grumbled as he struggled to sit erect, 'and don't spare the whiskey.'

West poured a stiff shot of Tennessee whiskey into a mug before filling the cup to the brim with hot, black coffee. He handed the steaming drink to his friend without a word, then sat patiently as the scout sipped the scalding liquid. After a few minutes, the mountain man seemed ready to talk.

'You got the trail yet?' Russell asked.

'Easy to follow.' West spoke in his soft, powerful voice, 'We'll catch up with 'em tomorrow.'

The old shootist made no effort to argue with the older man. He knew it would be pointless to try. While William Russell might need time to rest and recover, West knew the scout would not even consider such an arrangement. They would be on the trail before first light. Together, they would find the two professors and, the gunman grimly reflected, they would deal with the hardcase badmen who had left the trapper for dead along the trail to Palo Duro Canyon.

'How come you to be out along this trail?' Russell asked as he drained the mug. Before answering, West took the cup to fill it with a meat broth he had been simmering over the fire in anticipation of his friend's awakening. Regardless of how his stomach rolled at the thought, the old man knew he must eat. The broth would help him to regain his strength, so he simply accepted the cup and began to sip the thick broth while waiting for an explanation for his friend's presence so far from his home in the village of Spit Junction.

'Well, I followed up on a hunch,' West began, 'and it proved to be a good one.' The tall, silver-haired gunman settled down with another mug of coffee to sip as he talked. 'The mornin' you and them college fellers pulled out of town, another group of folks passed through Spit Junction. I steered clear of them boys cause I recognized right away they was badmen; the type that just might've recognized me. While I ain't never had no run in with them fellers personally, I knew Bill Malone and Len Holt from wanted posters, and the three hardcases that trailed along with 'em was nothin' more than saddle trash turned outlaw.' West continued his story while sipping the brew. Russell held out the empty mug for more of the meaty broth that now warmed his insides in a pleasant fashion. After refilling and returning the mug to his companion, the big gunman resumed his tale. 'Them boys picked up a few supplies at the general store, then had a couple of drinks over at the Emerald Palace Saloon before they headed on out of town.' West paused for a sip of coffee. 'But they asked questions. They asked O'Cooners about you and them professors...'

'So, you set out to foller along,' Russell finished the story. 'You think I'm gettin' too old to mind my own affairs, or you jist lookin' to mix up a little adventure?'

'Just thought you might want a little

company.' West shook his head in a solemn gesture, 'I'm too old for adventure.' He paused for a moment. 'So're you, old man.'

'You're right about that, son.' Russell lifted fingers to gently feel the bandage that covered the bullet crease along his scalp. 'I guess I was plenty lucky this time around.'

'I'd say so.' West handed the trapper another mug of coffee spiked with whiskey to finish off his meal. 'There was enough blood so's you looked near dead, but all the real damage was the bullet graze there and a bad nose bleed from falling off that tall black you been ridin'.'

Russell sipped the strong coffee with a smile of satisfaction before his face turned stern. 'They left me fer dead, boy.'

'I reckon they did at that.'

'I'll kill 'em when I find 'em.'

'I figgered as much, old man.' West's sky-blue eyes met the meadow-green ones across the dancing flames of the camp fire. 'I've had my fill of killin', Three Toes, but I'll back your play through to the end. We've got to git them two city dudes before Malone decides to kill 'em both.'

'Oh, we'll git Milly and Tilly back,' Russell assured the silver-haired shootist, 'and I'll take care of that Malone and his friends. I didn't git this old by lettin' trash sich as that cross my path more than once.' The trapper drained the warm coffee from the mug in a few final gulps before adding, 'I'm settling in fer the night now, son. We'll be up at it afore the sun.'

'Tomorrow.' West spoke the word as a promise before stretching out beneath his own blankets. From years of living by the gun, the big man knew what the coming day would bring. He could hear his companion's snores as he drifted off to dreamless sleep.

'Damn your dirty hides!' Malone raged at the professors as he stomped about waving the map above his head. 'Just what in the hell does this map say?'

The Malone gang was camped upon the floor of Palo Duro Canyon. A full day had passed since their attack upon Russell and the Easterners. Having stolen the map, kidnapped the professors, and left the old man for dead on the Staked Plains, they had negotiated a descent to the rugged canyon floor. After a day of searching for treasure and arguing over the map, Malone, Holt, and the others seemed no closer to finding the treasure than the day before.

'I can't make nothin' from all this here scribble-scrabble on this map!' Malone's frustration had boiled over into a fury. 'We're gonna have to make them two tell us what this is all about.'

'But they don't seem to want to talk.' Holt spoke softly, but a leering grin played over his features as he sat by the firelight nursing a cup of coffee. Night had fallen within the high canyon walls.

'Oh, they'll talk,' Malone growled an oath. 'I ain't gotten nasty with 'em yet, but now's the time to begin. We're gonna find out about that treasure tonight so's we can get to it first thing in the mornin'. That federal payroll is somewhere in this big ditch of canyon and we're gonna get it. Y'all hear me talkin' to you?' The outlaw glared at the captive college professors who seemed unconcerned with their predicament.

'We do hear you, Mr Malone,' Robertson responded, his bald head gleaming in the firelight of the night camp. 'The map instructions are written in Latin and I doubt very seriously if you will ever decipher their meaning. Besides that, there seems to be some confusion over the treasure that we are seeking. You see…'

'I see that I'm gonna have to play this thing all the way through to the finish.' Malone's tone left no doubt as to just how final the 'finish' would be for the two Easterners.

'Play however you like, Mr Malone,' Montgomery flatly stated, 'we have no intention of helping you locate the priceless treasure that we are seeking.'

'You'll help all right,' Malone snarled at the red-headed giant before turning his eyes to Holt. 'Heat up the knife blade, Len.'

115

The remaining three hardcases watched all that transpired with only whispered comments among themselves. Each knew what Malone and Holt had in store for the bound captives. For the past two years, these three badmen had travelled with the big outlaw chief and they had no doubts about what he now planned for the professors.

'Either of you two dudes ever seen what a hot blade can do to a man's face?' Malone asked with a leering grin while Len Holt knelt before the fire to hold the steel tip of a Bowie knife in the blaze. 'If the smell of burnin' flesh don't make you sick to your innards, then the pain will plumb drive you crazy.' Holt chuckled softly to himself as he shifted his gaze to the two men bound tightly and seated upon the ground before the one-eyed bandit, Malone continued his attempt at intimidation. 'The stink, fear, and pain don't even come close to what it'll do to your face. Not that you two is anything much to look at,' Holt and Malone laughed loudly at this attempt at humour,

116

'but by the time we slice and fry your faces, you'll be afraid to look in the mirror.'

'Do you rattle on all the time, old fellow?' Robertson spoke with an air of exaggerated boredom. 'I really do wish you would get on with the entertainment.'

'Indeed,' Montgomery grinned in response, 'I think the ugly brute just likes to hear himself talk. Of course, he has a receptive audience in the little monkey with the pistols.'

Holt stood up from beside the fire with an orange, glowing blade held before him. The little gunman kept his rage in check as he approached the professors who sat with easy smiles enlivening their features.

'There's been enough talkin' now,' the gunman's eyes glowed in anticipation. 'Time now to show you birds that we mean business.'

'You two think this is some kind of joke?' Malone scratched his head with some amazement at his prisoners. 'You got any idea what we got planned for you boys?'

'Shall we get on with it, gentlemen?' Robertson's words dripped with sarcasm. 'Don't hold up the show on our account.'

'Yes, please,' Montgomery interjected, 'do what you must,' his tone grew deadly serious, 'but we'll not let our treasure fall into the hands of such foul smelling creatures as yourselves.'

'Make no mistake about it, Mr Malone,' Robertson smiled, 'You'll never find that treasure without us.'

'And we have no intention of finding it with you,' Montgomery concluded. 'I believe we've said all that is necessary for the evening.'

'Hell,' Malone roared, 'you ain't even begun to talk!' The outlaw bossed dropped his hand to the grip of the .44 at his hip.

'No,' Holt cautioned, 'this is more fun, Bill.' He smiled a twisted grin as he brought the blade near Montgomery's face. 'We'll get some answers about that treasure before the night is over and,' the little gunman's eyes sparkled in the fire light, 'we'll have fun doin' it.'

BOOM!

A shot erupted from the darkness that surrounded the outlaw encampment. The Bowie knife seemed to leap from the gunfighter's hand. In a flash, Holt drew one of the short barrelled .45 pistols with his left hand while shaking the numb right in a futile effort to regain feelings in his fingers. Malone held the Remington .44 in his own fist. The outlaws stared out into the black night, but could find no target.

'Toss the weapons,' a voice boomed through the canyon. 'I'm comin' in.'

SIX

'Like hell I will,' snarled Malone while anger contorted his rugged features. 'You come on in here and we'll put a few extra holes in your no account hide. Who's out there in the dark anyhow?'

The one-eyed outlaw chief twisted his head about in an effort to see who might have fired the shot from outside the circle of firelight surrounding the small camp site. Len Holt stood very still, his right hand still stinging from the impact of the bullet that ripped the Bowie from his grasp. The little gunman's left hand held tightly to his Colt .45. He listened carefully for some sound of the unseen enemy. A slight noise could provide the killer with all he needed to place a lead slug in response. Malone might rage, and the other three might stare into the darkness, but Holt alone was truly prepared to kill.

'My name's Joshua Easterly,' the voice called from the night along the canyon floor. 'I own the hardware store back in Spit Junction.'

Holt shifted his balance to bring the revolver to bear upon the general direction from which the voice could be heard. However, he did not fire. Intuitively Malone's right-hand man knew that this man would not be so foolish as to speak from a position where he might be hit by a carefully fired shot in the dark. Holt remembered the old man from the Emerald Palace. The image of a hardcase cowboy slumping to the floor in a growing pool of scarlet flashed before the outlaw's mind. He held his fire.

'Come on in and let's talk,' Holt called out in response to the man he knew as Joshua Easterly. 'Maybe we can do a little business together.'

'We got no business,' the words carried determination, 'and you've got no more time; throw down those weapons or I'm gonna begin shootin' to kill. No more talk. No more time. Just do like I say.'

'He ain't kiddin', Bill,' Holt spoke softly. 'I've seen the old man in action and he can shoot.'

'Damn!' Malone muttered under his breath, then spoke aloud. 'Don't do nothin' crazy, mister!' Then, to Holt and the three members of his gang, 'Throw 'em down on the ground boys.'

Malone, Holt, and the remaining three badmen tossed their pistols to the earth. Each man was careful to see that the weapons remained within an easy distance, but, for now, the bandits were unarmed. Expressions ranged from smouldering rage on the part of Bill Malone to assured silence from his second-in-command.

'Your play now, Easterly,' Malone shouted.

'I'm comin' in,' West called out before stepping into the yellow glow of the dying camp fire blaze. The big, silver-haired gunman held the Colt Navy .36 in his right hand while the sky-blue eyes seemed everywhere at once. Even past sixty, the big man made an impressive figure in the cool, spring night as the glowing light flickered across his grim features. While Malone and the others mumbled curses beneath their breath, Holt looked on with a blank expression and remained quiet. He knew the nature of the man who held the upper hand. Holt did not fear the older man, but he had no doubt as to the deadly damage the .35 could manage. The hardware store man held the pistol with ease and comfort.

'Now what?' Malone growled the question. The one good hazel eye screamed hatred mixed with frustration.

'You can start by untying them two college dudes.' West's tone remained firm and steady. He left no question as to the implied threat if he was not obeyed.

No one moved for several seconds. Malone contemplated how close he must be to the treasure he sought, then let his gaze drift once more to the older man's face. He saw death in the blue eyes that almost seemed to glow by fire light.

'Do it!' The outlaw boss snarled the command to his three men. They moved as one, crossing from the opposite side of the fire before fumbling with the bonds that held Professors Robinson and Montgomery. In spite of their captivity, the two Three Toes had dubbed 'Milly' and 'Tilly' seemed healthy and happy.

'My goodness, so very good to see you, sir,' Robertson spoke with obvious good cheer as his hands were freed. 'I must say we've shared better company.'

'Indeed, we offer our sincere appreciation for your timely intervention on our behalf,' Montgomery's freckled face beamed with joy. 'So good of you to join us.'

'Just get yourselves ready to ride.' A slight grin animated the big man's features as he shook his head in disbelief over the Easterners' attitude. The odd couple rose to their feet rubbing at hands gone numb from the tight ropes.

'What you aimin' to do with us, old man?' Malone asked as concern began to temper his anger. 'We ain't wanted fer nothin' around here.'

'I might kill you.' The response seemed simple. There was not a trace of humour in the gunman's face or voice. 'That's what you'd do if you were in my place.'

'Hell, we ain't about to stand here while you...' The badman began his protest, but was cut short.

'Quiet!' West's tone silenced the outlaw as the sky-blue eyes met the hazel orb of the one-eyed bandit. 'I'm gonna let you all live, but I'm gonna tell you the honest truth. Listen and understand me, boys, cause this ain't no threat; just simple fact. If I ever see any of you again, then I'll kill you on sight.'

'You got no call to be so high and…' Malone blustered as his temper boiled out of control.'

'Don't rile me you two-bit owlhoot!' West let his own temper flare for a moment. 'I've killed better men than you in my time, and I'd do everybody concerned a favour if I left your dirty carcass rottin' out here for the coyotes to pick over. You'd best keep your mouth shut.'

Malone glared at the man with the pistol, but kept his silence. He could sense that this man called Easterly stood poised at the razor edge of violence. The three outlaws who had untied the professors looked away from the confrontation; afraid of being drawn into a showdown with the grim silver-haired figure. Len Holt looked on with interest.

'Just so you know,' the little man spoke softly now with no threat to his tone, 'I ain't scared of you.'

'That's too bad.' West's steady voice seemed to carry a note of sincere regret. 'Cause that probably means I'll have to kill you afore we wrap up this nasty business.'

'Or,' Holt let a faint smile play about his lips, 'I just might kill you.'

'Sometimes it works that way,' the old man admitted. Elijah West watched as the professors readied their horses for a departure. Each had their mounts as well as pack animals prepared for the trail.

'We await your direction sir.' Robertson grinned at his benefactor in the fading fire-light.

'At your service, 'Montgomery added.

'Let's ride.' West nodded toward the narrow pathway where his own horse waited a hundred yards away in the darkness. Before following the two professors who began to walk their mounts down the trail, he turned to face Len Holt one last time to speak a final prophecy; 'Some other time.'

'Wait!' Holt called out as the big man turned to follow the oddly matched pair into the surrounding night. 'Just who are you, mister?'

'A dead man.' West's reply came flat and emotionless from the dark, rocky pathway he had taken seconds before. 'Don't follow!' the warning echoed through the night in an almost ghostly whisper.

Silence gripped the camp for a full minute after the old shootist departed. The sound of horses had vanished. The badmen stood as if frozen in place in the orange glow of dying embers. Malone waited for some indication that they were being watched, then, finally, the camp erupted in activity.

'Get your guns!' Malone shouted. 'Let's get after that old devil! We got the map he's got the fellers than can read it.'

Each man scrambled for a gun and a horse. The scene would have been comical had the chaos not contained such deadly overtones. Before long the bandits would be armed, mounted and in pursuit of the old gunman and his well-educated charges.

BOOM!

A shot ran out through the night while a dark hole appeared above the right eye of one of the three outlaws who followed after Malone and Holt. The back of the man's head seemed to disintegrate as the lanky form fell forward into the glowing ashes of the camp fire. Sparks flew, but the figure did not move. The odor of smouldering flesh drifted through the area. The dead man's clothing burned while the others dropped to the ground with haste.

BOOM! BOOM!

One more of the three badmen hit the earth too late. Two lead slugs punched holes through his chest. The outlaw opened his mouth to scream, but only a gurgling sound emerged as crimson flowed forth. Crumpling to the rocky floor of the canyon, the man lay still as scarlet continued to pump from the holes to soak the ground beneath him. He was dead within seconds. The others waited for more shots to sound.

'You boys plannin' on goin' somewheres?' William Russell's gravel-voice called out from somewhere in the darkness. The old mountain man laughed at his own little joke. 'You fellers left me fer dead back along that trail, but I don't kill so easy now, do I?' His cackling chuckles filled the darkness.

BOOM!

The final of the three hardcase followers made a serious error in judgement. The man attempted to slip off into the night, but as he raised his head, Russell had snapped off a hasty shot that brought results similar to an exploding melon. The figure flopped to the ground in a pool of crimson and gore. The Malone gang members were all dead in less than a minute of deadly fire from the old man's Henry rifle.

'That sorta narrows the odds quite a bit,' the old scout called out with obvious delight. 'Now I ain't got time to play with you fellers. I've got business to attend to with old Milly and Tilly. Howsomever, I want you to know somethin' afore I leave you.' There was silence for a long minute as Malone and Holt kept their heads low with faces buried in the rocky soil. 'I'm gonna kill you both. Now, them three just made easy targets of themselves tonight, so's I'm done with them. Ain't got time to wait it out now, but I do hope you'll follow along after me so's we can git this thing over with soon. It don't really matter though, cause I'll kill you both when the time comes. So long now and,' the old man paused a moment, 'pleasant dreams, you filthy scalawags.'

Malone and Holt hugged the ground for an hour after Russell's final words. The old mountain man had killed three men they had ridden with for the past two years. He could still be out there with that big rifle ready to exact his revenge upon the two who remained alive. Neither man spoke during that interval. Instead, they simply waited. Waited and simmered with anger and frustration. After the hour elapsed, Malone muttered a curse before shifting his bulk to a sitting position upon the hard, rocky earth.

'He's gone,' the big outlaw spoke in a croaking whisper, his rage a barely controlled storm kept just beneath the surface. Like an active volcano, Bill Malone might erupt at any moment.

'Gone,' Holt echoed the outlaw leader's words as he scrambled to his feet. Guns in their holsters, the little man began a search for the big Bowie blade he had lost earlier in the evening.

'Let's get after that crew.' Malone trembled with repressed hostility as he carefully built a cigarette. Watching his companion retrieve the badly dented blade, the one-eyed outlaw scratched a Lucifer to flame in order to puff the tobacco to life. Blowing smoke through his nose, he continued, 'Them Easteners can't ride worth a damn; we can catch up to 'em in no time.'

'No.' Holt's voice remained calm.

'I'm still the boss of this outfit, Len!'

Malone glared at the man who had served as his right-hand in the gang that now lay sprawled about in various poses of death. 'We need to get on the trail while the gettin' is good.'

'There's no outfit any more, Bill,' Holt smiled faintly, 'but I'll allow as how you're still the boss. Just hear me out on this.'

Bad Eye Bill Malone let his hazel eye fall upon his old partner's face as he heaved a heavy sigh.

'What's on your mind, Len?'

'I think we need to give it a rest for the night.' Holt's face became thoughtful; his tone serious and cautious. 'We can follow along in the morning. No need for us to run off after those gunmen in the dark of night.'

'Why wait?' Malone's frustration exploded his composure. 'That only gives 'em more time to find our treasure.'

'Exactly,' Holt responded with deliberate assurance.

Understanding began to dawn upon Malone as he absorbed his partner's words.

Certainly, there was more than one way to go treasure hunting. Indeed, it might be easier to steal the federal payroll than to find it.

'Besides,' Holt continued, 'you know who I saw in that little town while I was there the other night?'

'Who's that?'

'Jasper Crenshaw.'

'You kiddin' me, Len?' Malone's features broke open in an ugly grin. Yellow teeth were exposed while the badman's eyes seemed to twinkle in the orange glow.

'He was there, big as life, Bill.'

'Where Jasper is,' the big outlaw laughed out loud, 'his brother Alfred ain't far behind.'

'That's right,' Holt replied. 'That would make the odds a little more to my liking.'

'Let's get away from the stink anyhow.' Malone's spirits had taken a decided turn for the better as he moved toward the remaining horses. The two outlaws would relocate away from the carnage left in the wake of the old trapper's rifle fire. The burned body still lay in the smouldering camp fire. The stench had become nearly unbearable. Malone and Holt would leave the dead for the coyotes of Palo Duro Canyon.

As Bill Malone and Len Holt prepared to move their camp for the evening, horses trotted through the night along a dark, narrow trail that wound through the canyon floor. The walls of the deep canyon cast black shadows while stunted trees lined the shallow stream that slipped along in silence. For another hour, the horses and men continued along the rocky pathway that followed the narrow thread of water. After a hard, two hour ride, West called a halt. Leading the horses in to a small, stone enclosure beside the trail, he dismounted and signalled for the professors to do the same.

'We'll spend the rest of the night here,' the shootist announced as he made to unsaddle the big bay he had ridden out from Spit Junction. 'These rocks make a natural fortress. I don't think Malone will follow us, but if he does we can sure hold him off from in here.'

'What about Mr Russell?' Robertson asked with concern. He stood beside his mount, bobbing his bird-like head in agitation. 'We really must find Mr Russell!'

'Indeed,' Montgomery joined in with his companion in their usual pattern, 'Mr Russell is injured out along the trail. Those bandits...'

A horse could be heard approaching at a rapid pace down the dark, narrow trail.

'That should be your Mr Russell about now.' West grinned at the two professors. Their faces gave evidence to the astonishment they felt in this moment of surprise. Old Three Toes rode his big charcoal into the small stone fortress that he and Elijah West had selected as their rendezvous earlier in the day.

'Well, I'll be dagblasted if it ain't old Dan'l Boone and Davy Crockett!' Russell winked at his old friend as he reined in the stallion before stepping lightly from the saddle. 'You hadn't give me up fer dead had you?'

'Heaven's no, Mr Russell,' Robertson

assured the old scout.

'Certainly not, Mr Russell,' Montgomery added.

'Good.' Three Toes began to unsaddle Jimmy. 'Then I suggest that Milly and Tilly here git a little sleep while we take turns keepin' a lookout through the night.'

'I heard shots.' West spoke softly as the Easterners unsaddled their horses and prepared to bed down for the remainder of the evening.

'Killed three of 'em afore I came along to join you,' Russell answered in a matter-of-fact tone. 'I didn't git Malone nor Holt, but I'll kill 'em later; sooner if they decide to foller us.'

West did not answer his friend. Although he had lived by his gun, he did not approve of killing except as a last resort. He could not help but wonder if Russell killed too easily these days. However, he knew it would do no good to argue with the old man. He had survived his many years on the frontier by living the hard life and following a rugged code that left no enemies alive to haunt your back trail. Russell had only let Malone and Holt live because of his concern for the professors and his obligation to West. He had wanted to rejoin the group to help Robertson and Montgomery achieve the goals of their expedition. After that, West knew the mountain man would track down the two outlaws and eliminate any threat they might pose for the future.

'We ain't seen the last of Malone and Holt,' West said as the professors stretched out upon their bed rolls. 'They won't give up this close to whatever it is they want.'

'That's what I'm hopin' fer, son.' Russell smiled in contentment as he pulled a blanket up to his whiskered chin. 'If they'll just cooperate by comin' along, then it'll save me the trouble of lookin' fer 'em when I'm done with Milly and Tilly. You jist keep watch and let me know if the varmints show up.'

Russell was asleep in seconds. The Easterners rested quietly while Elijah West sat comfortably in the boulders listening to the night sounds. A Panhandle showdown was on the way. The old shootist felt it deep in his bones. He only hoped that it would be his last.

SEVEN

The cluster of boulders protected the small group of campers from the winds that whipped through the deep canyon throughout the night. Elijah West had awakened his old friend a little before four o'clock, so sunrise found William Russell preparing breakfast before an open fire of aromatic mesquite wood. Bacon sizzled in a big iron skillet, biscuits began to rise in a covered pan, while coffee gurgled in a blackened pot. West had slept only a couple of hours, but he felt good waking up in the outdoors. A cool nip in the spring air greeted the old gunfighter as he threw off his blanket to struggle to his feet; joints creaked and popped their protests, but the big man soon stood tall in the grey light that preceded full dawn.

'Smells like you're ruinin' another meal, old man,' West called out to his companion. 'In all the years you've walked this earth I wonder that you've never learned to cook anything worth eatin'.'

Russell never looked up from the lean strips of bacon he forked about in the big skillet. 'I ain't never noticed you turnin' down my chow, Elijah, but if you've done got to be a picky eater then you can jist do without.'

West kept a straight face while shaking his head in outward resignation, 'Naw, I guess anything's better than nothin' at all.' The silver-haired gunman used a boot toe to nudge the sleeping figure of Professor Robertson. The big man knew that old Three Toes remained one of the best trail cooks west of the Mississippi. The old man could make biscuits that would melt in a man's mouth. However, he never would admit as much to Russell's face. Again, he prodded the sleeping man with the toe of a scuffed boot.

'Good morning,' Robertson bobbed his bird-like head as he popped up to a sitting position. 'An absolutely splendid day to be sure!'

'Yes, indeed,' Montgomery picked up the theme of his colleague's remarks, 'I'd say we have a wonderful day before us for our expedition.' The big professor ran a freckled hand through his wiry red hair that seemed to stick out in all directions.

'Mornin', gentlemen,' West offered a cheerful greeting. 'If you can stomach it, then that dried up excuse for a mountain man has some grub on the fire. Let's eat.'

'Git it afore it gits cold!' Three Toes growled out his command as the others assembled around the small blaze. The camp fire took the chill from the cool Panhandle morning. As they enjoyed the bacon and biscuits, Russell, at last, made introduction, including a few words of explanation regarding Elijah

West, his background, and current identity. The professors made no response except to nod their heads in understanding. A satisfied silence settled over the four as the meal continued. Each had seconds heaped high on their plates while the stringy, leather-tough old Russell managed to get down yet a third serving as well.

The professors looked on in amused bewilderment while the old trapper wiped his plate clean of bacon grease with a final, fluffy biscuit. In one simple gesture, the scout stuffed the treat into his mouth with a contented sigh of happiness. A grinning West made no effort to conceal his own humour at his companion's appetite. 'I knowed this old goat for almost forty years.' The gunman shook his silver head as he addressed the professors. 'And I still can't figure where all the chow goes on them skinny bones.'

'Never you worry,' Russell winked at Robertson and Montgomery, 'a little good grub is what we all need afore we set out lookin' fer them old elephink bones. Ain't that right, Milly and Tilly?'

'Indeed,' Robertson nodded in agreement, 'a delightful breakfast, Mr Russell.'

'Certainly,' Montgomery affirmed, 'I've never tasted finer. I'm ready for the trail, Mr Russell.'

Each man now savoured a final cup of steaming, black coffee as they surveyed their surroundings. Palo Duro Canyon had to be one of the most beautiful settings on earth. By first light, the canyon's varied colours could be easily discerned. Orange, gold, brown, red, grey and white, the layers of the canyon walls evidenced multiple shades as they rose to a height of some eight hundred feet above their heads. Beyond their small stone fortress, sage brush yucca, mesquite and cedar trees were scattered along the strip of water known as Palo Duro Creek or, as it was sometimes called, the 'Prairie Dog Town' Fork of the Red River. The new days' bright orange sun played about the canyon walls while the four men looked on in awe at the indescribable natural wonder.

'After all these years,' Russell broke the silence to observe, ' I still never get used to finding this big, beautiful ditch right smack in the middle of the flat, open Panhandle plains.'

West nodded his head in agreement. 'You'd sure never expect to see such a sight as this. I've ridden the length of the whole thing once or twice before. It runs more'n a hundred miles through these high plains, and that's a fact.'

'Without a doubt, it is one of the most marvellous landscapes I have ever experienced.' Robertson's tone seemed a reverent whisper.

'A magnificent display of nature at her finest.' Montgomery remained overwhelmed by his surroundings as the coffee turned cold in the tin cup he held loosely in his grip.

For a few moments more, West and Russell allowed the Easterners to enjoy the canyon's scenery; then Three Toes scrambled to his feet to clean up from their meal. Tossing dirt upon the camp fire, Russell growled a good natured question to his old trail companion.

'You gonna sit around all mornin' or git them horses saddled, packed, and ready to move out?'

'I'm movin'.' West quickly rose to his feet to prepare for the day's ride. Before moving toward the horses, he met Robertson's gaze. 'You two better figure out just where it is you want to go. Unless I miss my guess, Malone and Holt will turn up before we wrap this business up. The sooner we find your old bones, the better off we'll all be.' The old gunman turned on his heel without waiting for a response. The professors proceeded with a vigorous discussion regarding the directions outlined in the old map.

Packed, saddled, and ready for the trail, West and Russell stood before the professors in something less than twenty minutes with expectant looks upon their faces.

'You might recall that the outlaw chief, Malone, has possession of our map,' Robertson began. The pith helmet shaded his eyes while his nose protruded, beak-like, from the shadows. His adam's apple bounced up and down as he spoke. 'We refused to translate the map's notations for the scoundrel, but the old boy does have the map.'

'Of course,' Montgomery hastened to add, 'we recall the basics of that document. We believe,' his freckled face split wide with a happy grin, 'that with a little trial and error, we will be able to locate the site we seek. Lovely day for a pleasant ride through the canyon.'

Both men were in such obvious high spirits that neither West nor Russell had the heart to be pessimistic over their chances of locating the prehistoric fossils. All mounted their horses to proceed along the canyon floor away from their evening camp site and in the opposite direction from their encounter with Malone's outlaw band.

Riding easily along the trail, Robertson queried, 'Palo Duro translates to "hard wood", does it not?'

'That's right,' Russell replied. 'Injuns used

to come here to gather up them hard cedar branches fer their bows and arrows. The canyon took the name from that.' The old man's eyes never rested as he scanned the trail before them for any sign of danger; West did the same.

'Are there still Indians in the area?' Montgomery questioned the old scout with no hint of fear in his voice. 'I'd love to meet some of the local natives.'

'Ain't many Injuns here about no more,' the guide spoke with a touch of sorrow to his voice. 'MacKenzie and the cavalry whipped the fire out of the Comanche back in '74 right here in this canyon. Now old Charlie Goodnight runs cattle down here on the JA Ranch. Hell, this ditch covers more'n 15,000 acres. There's plenty of room fer sure.'

'I hear tell Goodnight has a fair size herd of buffalo runnin' loose in Palo Duro too.' West shot a glance toward his old partner while a grin played about his lips. 'Couple hundred head or more around these parts.'

'Ain't had no buffler steaks in a long, long

time.' The mountain man let his pink tongue moisten dry lips. 'You reckon we might run across some them big critters down along this trail?'

'If we don't find no buffalo, then there's always quail around about,' West assured his old friend. 'Always plenty of quail, rattlers, and lizards.'

'Not to mention coyotes!' Russell laughed out loud at the puzzled looks that passed across the faces of the professors. 'Don't worry, boys, we ain't about to make y'all eat no rattlers, lizards, nor coyote meat. Although,' he winked at Elijah West, 'there's been plenty of times in the past fifty years that I've had worse. Howsomever, somewhere's down the way here we'll rustle us up some fine quail or,' again the pink tongue slurped across his lips, 'if we're lucky you'll be sinking your teeth into a big, juicy slab of buffler!'

'I am always open to new experiences, Mr Russell,' Robertson's head bobbed about on his spindly neck.

'Certainly willing to give it a try.' Montgomery's freckled face beamed his agreement while West and Russell simply grinned with anticipation of the coming meal.

Several hours passed in the saddle. Robertson and Montgomery paused often to confer regarding their general direction while Russell took the lead in selecting particular trails and pathways. All routes wound along the rocky canyon floor between clumps of boulders, towering mesas, and clusters of mesquite and cedar trees. Generally, they followed along beside the murky-brown, shallow stream that they had camped near the night before. Losing sight of the ribbon of water from time to time, all trails seemed to find the way back to the twisting, cool creek as they crossed and recrossed this branch of the Red River again and again through the long morning on horseback.

'We gittin' any closer to where we's headed?' Russell had removed his old fur cap to scratch his head. West stood nearby in a small patch of shade provided by a gnarled cedar tree. All had dismounted while the horses dipped their muzzles into the refreshing water of Palo Duro Creek. The sun hung high over the canyon now but had already begun to slip toward the western horizon. 'I'm too old to be chasin' all over the Palo Duro lookin' fer old bones. You two had best know where we're goin' and git us there fast.'

West let his sky-blue eyes meet those of his oldest friend. 'I'm less concerned about your old bones than I am meetin' up with Malone down one of these narrow trails.'

Three Toes evidenced a wide grin that split his face from ear to ear. 'You let me worry about that one-eyed snake. He slipped away from me once, but I'll not let the sorry scalawag git away…'

The scout stopped in mid-sentence. He felt the rumble beneath his moccasined feet. The rocky soil began to vibrate as the mountain man's meadow-green eyes lit up with excitement.

'Dinner's on the way, old man,' the silver-haired gunman called out as he mounted his horse. 'Let's get these two dudes a robe to keep 'em warm up there in them cold Maine winters.'

'You couldn't hit a buffler if you was ridin' on his back!' Russell exclaimed with delight as he swung lightly into the saddle upon Jimmy's back. The big charcoal seemed eager for the chase.

'Mr Russell...' Robertson began.

'Mr West...' Montgomery's question was lost as he watched the big man touch heels to his horse and set off at a gallop toward the sound of thunder.

'You two wait there,' Russell jabbed a finger in the direction of a small cluster of rocks and scattered, large boulders. 'We'll be back directly with buffler.'

With no more time for words, Russell quickly turned Jimmy into the wake of Elijah West. The black caught up with the shootist so both friends were off in the direction of the pounding hooves of the buffalo herd. Within minutes they had climbed their horses near the top of a rocky rise where they dismounted to continue on foot. A short time later, the two companions were lying prone upon the hill looking down upon the small herd of shaggy beasts that stretched across the canyon floor before them. The buffalo had ceased their brief run in order to graze among the sage and yucca plants. Some waded out into the muddy creek.

'What do you suppose spooked 'em into that run?' West spoke in a whisper as he gazed out upon the big, brown creatures that now seemed at peace in the Palo Duro.

'No tellin',' Russell shot back. 'They's touchy critters. One thing's fer sure though, they's still enough now, Elijah. Hell, even you ought to be able to hit one of 'em from this distance.'

'Almost like the old days.' The gunman had a faraway look in his eyes for a passing moment.

'No, son,' the scout shook his head sadly, 'in the old days, they was thousands of the big shaggies. There's no more'n a couple 'hundred or so of the beasts down there now.'

'Almost seems a shame to shoot one,' West spoke as he brought the Winchester saddle gun to bear just behind the shoulder of a small cow that stood some hundred and fifty yards away, nibbling at a green shoot sticking from the rocky soil. 'Almost,' he added softly.

Russell levelled the big Henry upon another of the shaggy brutes with a weary grin. 'Ain't gonna make no difference now, son. We might as well eat good tonight and let Milly and Tilly take back a couple of buffler robes to show off to their college friends back east.'

BOOM! BOOM!

Each man squeezed gently upon the trigger of the long gun he held. Each man put a shot through the heart and lungs of a buffalo. Puffs of dust rose with a thud as the lead struck home. The animals took a few steps before stumbling to the earth with a bellow. The remainder of the herd stormed off down the canyon, lost to sight in the passing of a few brief moments.

'Come on, son!' Russell had already scrambled down the rocky rise to reunite with Jimmy. 'We got skinning, butcherin' and cookin' to do!'

Elijah West followed close behind.

Evening found Russell, West, Robertson, and Montgomery feasting upon roasted buffalo steaks before a warm camp fire. Coyotes howled as the moon rose above the canyon, and that same moon looked down upon another small camp some few miles distance.

'Len told you boys the score in town.' Malone ate peaches from a can as he let his hazel eye fall upon the two newcomers. 'There's plenty for all of us when we get our hands on that federal payroll.'

'They know what we're after, Bill,' Len assured the outlaw boss while puffing a cigarette. The burning tobacco glowed orange in the darkness. Both Malone and Holt examined the recent reinforcements to their outlaw band.

Jasper Crenshaw stood close to six feet, with two hundred and fifty pounds well distributed about his heavy frame. Greasy, black hair, streaked with grey, hung shabby about his shoulders. A dirty plaid shirt strained to contain his well-muscled torso while patched denim jeans were cuffed above scuffed, dusty boots. A perpetual scowl twisted the ugly, unshaven face. A slouch-brim, shapeless brown hat concealed his eyes in dark shadows. A bulky Smith and Wesson Schofield .45 stuck out from the waist of the big man's pants, while the grip of a smaller .38 calibre pistol jutted from a bulging left-hand pant's pocket. Dirty, calloused hands held tight to a sawed-off American Arms 12 gauge shotgun. Jasper's twin brother, Alfred, stood close by in the darker shadows behind his sibling. Like Jasper, Alfred bristled with weapons and scowled at Malone. The Crenshaw brothers favoured the destructive power of the short-barrelled shotguns, but carried pistols for back up fire power. The men preferred to be left alone. However, they had been unable to turn down the offer of a cut in the long-lost Briscoe treasure. They did not like Malone nor Holt. The little gunfighter had risen before daylight and pushed his mount hard to reach Spit Junction by early after-noon. He had approached the brothers and they had immediately agreed to return with him to Palo Duro Canyon. Now, late in the evening, Bad Eye Bill Malone had a gang ready for action.

'We all agreed on an even split?' The one-eyed bandit asked as he attempted to fasten upon the eyes hidden beneath the sagging brim of that frayed brown hat.

Jasper Crenshaw only nodded once in reply.

'Let's sleep on it,' Malone grinned. The gesture seemed vulgar as the yellowed teeth of the outlaw reflected the fire light. 'We'll be rich by this time tomorrow night.'

A coyote yipped in the distance to be answered by a long, mournful howl from another rocky peak. The moon hung high in the night sky as darkness gripped the Palo Duro. With no further conversation, the badmen settled down for a few hours' sleep.

EIGHT

Sunlight spilled over the rim of Palo Duro Canyon. The new day found the professors, along with their two guides, seated around another small camp fire some twenty odd miles from the previous night's stopping place. The four companions had spent a comfortable evening in a clearing near the creek that wound through the canyon floor. Expecting an eventful day, all were up before daylight for a buffalo steak breakfast complete with fluffy biscuits and thick gravy. The men now reclined about the dwindling blaze in postures of contented relaxation as they enjoyed a final cup of hot, black coffee. Tin mugs steamed in the cool morning air while the men surveyed the delightful variety of colours brought forth by the rising sun. Dawn was a beautiful time of day in the ancient canyon.

While the Easterners seemed oblivious to all but the grandeur of their surroundings, Elijah West knew that the day held a promise as well as a threat. The promise of locating the sought after prehistoric bones seemed more than off-set by the threat that Malone would catch up to them sooner or later. The longer they remained in the canyon, West reflected, the greater their danger from the bandit. One thing for certain, the gunman let a faint smile play about his lips, it would be an eventful day.

'It jist don't git no better than buffler and biscuits fer breakfast.' Three Toes expressed his satisfaction over the morning meal while rubbing his hard, flat stomach with a lather-tough palm. 'I declare that's some good eatin'.'

'My compliments to the chef,' Robertson

spoke up with a broad smile giving life to his sunny disposition. 'Today's menu even surpasses the superb dinner we consumed with enthusiasm this past evening.'

'Without a doubt,' Montgomery joined in the praise for Russell's skill with outdoor cooking. 'I have never tasted finer selections of meat under any circumstances, Mr Russell; a marvellous meal to be sure.'

'These boys don't get around much.' West concealed a grin as he finished off his coffee. 'I've had better grub from the free lunch counter of a ghost town saloon.'

Russell turned to his old friend with a sneer to his lips. 'I suppose that's why you helped yourself to an extry plate full of everything.'

The big gunman shook his head. 'No, I was just afraid of leaving that slop lying about here in the open. Sure 'nuff don't want to poison no innocent coyotes.'

'Elijah West, I've had about enough of your dagblasted foolishness for one mornin'. Now, you git yourself up from here so's we can git out on the trail afore we waste the day lollygagging aroun' this here fire.'

'I'm movin', old man,' West chuckled softly as he scrambled to his feet. He turned toward the horses, but Robertson's call interrupted his progress.

'Excuse me, please, Mr West,' Robertson's head bobbed vigorously so that his enormous ears seemed to flap. His smile almost consumed his entire face. 'We have an announcement to make.'

'A most welcome announcement I might add.' Montgomery's own freckled face split wide with good humour.

'We believe the treasure to be near this very spot!' The little professor shook his head with excitement.

'Quite near, quite near,' Montgomery assured the others with obvious enthusiasm.

'After much deliberation and consultation, Professor Montgomery and I have reached the conclusion that the fossilized remains of a prehistoric mastodon...'

'That's an old hairy elephink in case you didn't know, son,' Russell informed West

159

with a wink and a grin.

Robertson only nodded and smiled at the interruption. 'We believe the remains to be located within a mile radius of this very camp site.'

Montgomery pulled the pith helmet over his wiry red hair. 'It is our intention to locate the site and begin our preliminary excavations this very morning.'

'Let's git at it then, gents!' Russell drained the coffee from his battered tin mug in one final swallow. 'I ain't never seen no elephink bones, so's I'm ready as I'll ever be.'

After cleaning up from their morning meal, West secured the horses before the four men set out on foot to explore the surrounding area. The cool morning air had made way to a warm spring day, but the expedition proceeded without pause in spite of the climbing sun. Only a few hours had passed when about mid-morning, the professors suddenly stopped still as if frozen in place upon the narrow trail. West and Russell came to a halt close behind the two statue-like figures who now blocked the dusty pathway. The two old companions waited in expectant silence as the Easterners examined the clearing before them. A flat stretch of rocky soil covered an area of fifty yards square, sparse sage and yucca scattered the ground. To the right ran the muddy, shallow waters of Palo Duro Creek, lined by dense brush along with cedar and mesquite. On the left, boulders and rock lay in chaotic heaps at the foot of the sheer canyon wall. In the absolute centre of the clearing sat a large misshapen cedar with twisted, gnarled limbs. In the highest branch of that tree rested an immense buffalo skull. Robertson and Montgomery fixed their eyes upon that skull with satisfaction. Joy radiated from the faces of the professors as they turned to speak to their new found friends.

'Gentlemen, this is the location!' Robertson announced to all interested parties. 'This is the missing element that Mr Malone needed translated from the Latin. Our old colleague from the college had described this exact site in his Latin phrases while only indicating the general area on the map he sketched by hand. We are prepared to proceed with our work immediately in the area beneath the skull.'

'There is no doubt about it,' Montgomery agreed. 'We have located the remains of an ancient mastodon. We are simply left with the task of uncovering the skeleton.'

'How long ago was that other feller here?' Three Toes asked the professors now that they had begun to unpack a variety of tools from the canvas bags each carried about their shoulders. 'I mean the one what made that map you boys got a holt of fer this little trip.'

'The previous expedition to this area occurred shortly before the unpleasant confrontation between the various states.' Robertson replied as he continued to pull implements from the large pack where his attention remained focused.

'The war between the states,' Montgomery clarified for West and Russell.

'I figgered it out, Tilly,' Three Toes remarked with sarcasm directed at the large, freckled face of Professor Montgomery. Returning his gaze to the bird-like Robertson, he observed, 'That was a long time ago, Milly. Hell, there's been a good deal happen aroun' these parts in all them years.'

'I hardly figure the critter got up and walked away, old man.' West grinned as he watched the professors hurry over to begin the careful digging beneath the skull that hung high in the twisted, grey branches of the dead cedar tree. 'If that old fossil was here all them years, then I suppose they'll find them bones just where that other college man left 'em back before the war.'

'Probably will at that.' Russell shook his head in agreement as he and his companion settled to the earth to watch Robertson and Montgomery attend to their task with the joy, enthusiasm, and satisfaction that accompanies hard work of a productive nature.

West and Russell watched as the odd couple worked throughout the warm morning and into the middle of the afternoon. The old scout and the silver-haired gunman had many shared experiences with which to pass the time in conversation. The big man whittled a cedar branch with a small fold-up knife extracted from his jeans while the trapper talked of old days and old ways. Long years on the frontier had taught the two to enjoy good companionship when available for there were always long months alone.

Meanwhile, Robertson and Montgomery chattered endlessly as they used picks, shovels, and a variety of smaller tools to dig holes. They worked carefully, but quickly beneath the gnarled limbs of cedar. Stopping only for half an hour around noon to sip some water and nibble at a cold, leftover biscuit, the professors seemed hardly to have broken a sweat in spite of the sun's warmth. After this brief delay, they returned to the growing pit with renewed energy. Work had slowed in the past hour as the Easterners spent most of the time on hands and knees in a hole now some three feet deep and six by eight feet in size. Tools littered the area surrounding the excavation site while the two men's chattering voices could be heard without a break. Little more than two pith helmets and an occasional posterior could be identified as the men worked at their task. At long last, they called out to the others.

'Mr West! Mr Russell! Come quickly!' Robertson's voice called out in excitement, his head lifted over the rim of their large hole in order to meet the gaze of the two older men seated some fifteen yards away.

'Please, do come and see, gentlemen,' Montgomery invited as he brought his freckled face above the lip of the big ditch the two had dug through the day. 'It is a remarkable discovery to be sure.'

West rose to his feet before extending a helping hand to Russell who accepted this assistance without comment. The two friends ambled easily over to the side of the shallow pit to gaze down upon the professors and their find.

'What've you got down there, Milly and Tilly?' Russell asked casually as he strolled to the edge. 'You done found your elephink?'

'Indeed, Mr Russell,' Robertson spoke with pride.

'Certainly,' echoed Montgomery. 'A marvellous discovery!'

'Well, I'll be sheep dipped!' the old trapper exclaimed as he stared down into the pit. 'Double sheep dipped!'

'That's a sight to behold.' West shook his head in awe.

'You done said a mouthful, son,' the mountain man commented. 'I jist never thought it would be that big!'

The professors sat upon the far edge of the rocky pit while West and Russell examined their impressive find. Clearly evident at this point in the excavation were the large skull and tusks of the great beast that had once been an immense, woolly, prehistoric mammoth. Other bones stretched back from the huge skull in some disarray. All of these skeletal remains were only partially uncovered, but what could be seen left everyone present in a state of amazed silence for long minutes. Even a retired gun-fighter and a crusty trapper could app-reciate the importance of these old bones. Eventually, West broke the silence with a question. Pointing off to the side, the big man spoke in soft, even tones.

'What's that down on the far side there about a foot beneath the surface?' He indicated an object protruding from the wall of the pit toward the centre of the pre-historic creature's disassembled remains. 'See it? There where the critter's back would be if he still had a back.'

'Yes, yes, we noticed it, Mr West. We've been trying to work around it.' Robertson nodded his head with mild annoyance. 'It appears to be some old chest or strong box of some sort.'

'It has no bearing upon your expedition, Mr West,' Montgomery added. 'There's certainly no need for us to be concerned with it.'

'Dig it up,' the old gunman spoke softly, but his eyes grew hard. Something seemed to crawl down the big man's spine.

'Really, Mr West, we simply...' Robertson protested.

'Dig it up!' West demanded once more.

'But, Mr West, we really must...' Montgomery began.

'Git on with it, Milly and Tilly.' Russell's green eyes carried a puzzled expression, but he recognized the serious nature of his friend's demand. 'Elijah here tells you to git that big box out of your hole, then jist start diggin' and pull the thing out of there. Ain't no point in arguing over it, boys.'

With only a temporary loss of their customary good humour, the professors went to work with pick and shovel to extract the heavy, iron chest from the surrounding earth. After an hour's labour, the two men brought forth a black box that demanded their best efforts to lift from the shallow pit. A large, tarnished brass padlock clattered against the iron as the chest banged to the hard earth outside the hole. This task completed, both men now seemed satisfied to have the obstructing item clear of the Mastodon bones.

'Delighted to have that old relic out of our way,' Robertson's smile threatened to split his face in two.

'Indeed,' Montgomery spoke with pleasure, 'this clears the way to continue with our excavation.'

'Hold up a minute.' West knelt before the black iron box to scrape dirt from the area just above the old brass padlock. 'This here is a federal government box.' His efforts had revealed the letters and symbols of an official United States treasury chest.

'Well, I'm dagblasted fer a sheep lover!' Russell exclaimed. 'Just what in tarnation do you think...'

'We'll take the box!' a voice boomed out over the clearing. 'Get clear of that chest, put your hands up over your heads, and don't nobody do nothin' stupid!'

From the brush that fronted the stream stepped the big one-eyed outlaw boss, Bill Malone. Beside him walked the little gunman with twin Colt pistols, Len Holt. Neither man had drawn their weapons; a testament to Malone's confidence in Holt and to Holt's own confidence in his speed and skills with the short-barrelled .45 revolvers strapped about his hips. However, the most important factor in this Panhandle showdown seemed to be the Crenshaw brothers, who approached the excavation pit from the litter of rocks and boulders along the base of the canyon wall. Jasper and Alfred held the deadly shotguns with stubby, double barrels trained upon West and Russell. The grim expression on the twin's faces made it clear that they had no reservations about pulling the triggers. Roberson and Montgomery sat quietly as they were all but ignored by the hardcase outlaws that closed in upon those assembled near the strong box.

'Just keep them hands high and step away

from that there big, iron box,' Malone snarled the command. West and Russell retreated from the chest with hands held above their shoulders. The professors now scrambled from their hole to stop on the opposite side of the pit from their companions. The Easterners stood within a few feet of the deadly Crenshaw brothers. 'You boys done found our treasure for us!' the bandit announced. He then snapped a demand at his second in command. 'Get that lock off a there, Len!'

BOOM!

No one present could follow the gunman's speed as he slipped the pistol from his holster, fired, and returned the weapon home all in one fluid motion. One shot and the lock hung shattered upon the latch of the old iron box.

'That's fine, Len.' Malone actually drooled in anticipation of possessing the contents of the chest. 'Go ahead. Flip that lid open. We'd all like to gander at the goods.'

Holt used a polished boot toe to kick open

the heavy iron lid. The long closed hinges shrieked in rebellion, but slowly the top raised to reveal a small fortune in silver, gold, and federal currency. Malone and Holt shouted for joy while the Crenshaw brothers kept their eyes and shotguns upon West and Russell.

'You know what this is?' Malone let his hazel eye meet those of the old scout. 'You got any idea what's in that there box, your ornery old coot?'

Russell scowled at the bandit. 'I can see it you dagblasted, fool. I ain't blind.'

'It's the old Briscoe loot.' West's tone was matter-of-fact. 'I had a hunch that's what you boys was after when you passed through Spit Junction. Folks've been lookin' for this old federal payroll since the reconstruction days just after the war. It was only a matter of time before somebody came across it. Seems the Briscoes found this old skull in the cedar tree to be a good marker and buried their treasure right on top of these old bones. Between the map you got, and the trail the professors left, I'd say you're a lucky man. I suppose this will make you and the rest of these boys as rich as they come.'

'I'd sure 'nuff say you're right about that, Pappy!' Malone's confidence in his control over the situation allowed him the luxury of a wide grin that exposed chipped, yellow teeth. 'Now, what do you suppose that makes you and your pals here, Grandpa?'

'I wouldn't want to make a guess on that score,' West let his sky-blue eyes meet that of the outlaw boss, 'but I'd be real careful about what you do from here.'

Russell's eyes flashed green fire. 'I'd hate to see you scalawags make any hasty decisions. You jist might come to regret 'em afore we was finished with you.'

'Listen here, you old mountin' goat,' Malone growled on oath, 'I done left you for dead once. The mistake I made was in not seeing the job done proper.' The one-eyed bandit chief let his big fists clench into tight balls at his sides. 'You shot up my gang night before last. Now, we've got the treasure and you're all gonna die.'

'Better men than you have made that threat.' Russell spat in the direction of Malone's boots. 'I'll dance on your grave you one-eyed plug-ugly!'

Malone's face turned an unhealthy crimson as he fought to control his rage. At last a confident grin returned to his battered features.

'Jasper and Alfred,' Malone spoke softly in a voice that seemed to rumble up from his depths. 'Save the two college fellers to pack and load the loot for us. Them other two,' he indicated West and Russell with a nod, 'they's too dangerous to have about. Kill 'em!'

NINE

'One moment, please, Mr Malone!'

Professor Robertson's hairless skull bobbed about on his slender neck as he wiped a thin hand across his shiny dome. Allowing his discarded pith helmet to fall to the ground near his feet, the scholarly little men interrupted the executions of West and Russell with a polite, but firm tone of voice.

'Are we to understand that it is your intention to do bodily harm to our companions?' Robertson's features were stern and disapproving. 'We really cannot condone such conduct.'

'Indeed!' Professor Montgomery's freckled face showed strong resolve. 'Please, do clarify your plan of action in this matter if you would be so kind.'

The Crenshaw brothers never took their eyes from the intended victims. Perpetual scowls made it impossible to know the thoughts of the twins, but the sawed-off barrels pointed toward West and Russell left little doubt as to their intentions.

Malone and Holt stared at the two professors with complete bewilderment blanketing their faces. Scratching at his stubbled chin with dirty, broken nails, the one-eyed outlaw managed a response through sneering lips.

'We plan to have Jasper and Alfred there,' he nodded in the direction of the shotgun men who stood close by the Easterners, 'blow holes through 'em and then leave their bodies for the buzzards. What the stink birds don't eat by day, the coyotes will finish up come dark.'

'That simply will not do.' Robertson shook his bird-like head in the negative. His eyes met the blood-shot hazel orb of the big hardcase without blinking. 'I'm afraid we cannot allow such activity to progress.'

'Certainly not, Mr Malone.' Montgomery's voice carried strong conviction. 'I do believe that the best course of action for all concerned would be for you to pack up and move along as quickly as possible.'

'You think it's that easy?' The bandit chief stared at the professors with a puzzled expression. He wiped his nose with a stained shirt sleeve before continuing. 'You think all you got to do is tell me to move along and we'll just hop on our ponies and be gone!'

'We've come a long way for this money.' Holt joined in the conversation now. The diminutive gunman allowed himself a small measure of amusement as his lips curled in a dangerous grin. 'We ain't about to leave here without that old Briscoe treasure. There's enough there for us to live like kings!'

'By all means, gentlemen,' Robertson's face brightened, 'do take the box along with you. We have no claim upon your treasure. You are welcome to it.'

Montgomery allowed his freckled face a cautious grin. 'We have no interest at all in that old chest nor the lost payroll. Carry it off, but please do be on your way. We have a great deal of work to do.'

Jasper and Alfred Crenshaw seemed oblivious to all the talk. The twins kept their eyes, as well as their shotguns, trained upon the big gunman and the dirty old scout. West and Russell kept their hands above their heads while watching the verbal exchange with befuddled amazement.

'Let's get this over with.' Holt almost

whispered the suggestion to his long-time boss. 'I don't see no point to all this crazy talk with these dudes.'

'Len's right,' Malone growled. 'I've had enough out of you two city boys. Now, keep your mouths shut while we get on with the job!'

'Are we to assume then that you refuse some reasonable compromise in this matter?' His shining pate reflected sunlight as the professor's head wobbled about in obvious agitation.

'Will you not be satisfied with anything short of killing Mr West and Mr Russell?' Montgomery's features had resumed their mask of firm resolve. 'Is there no way for us to avoid a violent conclusion to this awkward situation?'

'We're wastin' time!' Holt snarled.

'I told you two to...' Malone began a threat, but his words were cut short by the little professor.

'They leave us no choice in the matter, Professor Montgomery.' Robertson shook his head solemnly. His eyes evidenced sincere regret. 'We shall be forced to take immediate action.'

'No choice in the matter at all, Professor Robertson,' Montgomery agreed with grim determination. 'We must protect our friends from harm.'

As Malone and Holt looked on in the silence of confusion the two professors burst into action. The Crenshaw brothers stood within a few feet of the Easterners, so they had easy access to the deadly shotguns that threatened the lives of their companions. Without any hint of fear, the fragile Professor Milton T. Robertson moved swiftly to disable the hardcase closest to him. His left hand latched firmly upon the barrel of the shotgun held by Alfred Crenshaw. With surprising strength he tugged the weapon's business end toward the earth while his right hand darted to a large pocket of his baggy trousers. In a flash that hand emerged grasping a Remington Over-and-Under .41 which he immediately pressed against his opponent's temple with a surprisingly steady hand. Robertson's simple command, 'Drop it!' sounded convincing to Alfred who suddenly let the big 12-gauge fall to the earth with a clatter.

Meanwhile, the larger, younger Professor Tillery J. Montgomery swung a big, freckled fist that connected with Jasper's jaw. The force of the unexpected blow caused the big outlaw to lose his grip upon the stubby-barrelled shotgun. The fearsome weapon fell to the rocky ground. Jasper stumbled backward a few paces and a tiny worm of blood crawled from his lower lip. For a moment, Jasper stood in silence letting his tongue lick at that crimson stain. The big man's eyes blazed hatred. His fists clenched to form giant, hairy mallets at his sides.

'Give it to 'im Jasper!' Holt goaded the man into activity from across the shallow excavation pit.

'Kill 'im with your bare hands!' Malone snarled with blood lust glaring from his hazel eye.

Before anyone else could speak or act, Jasper let out an enraged bellow as he charged forward swinging a massive right fist at the head of Professor Montgomery. The pith helmet sailed some fifteen feet across the clearing to land in a clump of sage. However, the freckled professor had ducked beneath the force of the blow. Crouched low, Montgomery planted a series of blows to his opponent's mid-section that brought an explosion of foul breath. The bulky giant staggered back several steps in pain and frustration. Seizing the advantage, the Easterner moved in behind a stiff leg jab to land a big, over-hand right that rocked Jasper Crenshaw back upon his heels.

'I trust that this will sufficiently demonstrate my point...' Montgomery paused to lecture his opponent, but was interrupted by a bestial roar from the big hardcase that stood before him. The fight was far from over.

Jasper stormed forward faking another round-house right then connecting with a left upper-cut as Montgomery ducked the punch. That blow split the professor's lips to bring forth a shower of scarlet as he sat down hard in the sage. The outlaw grinned as he brought up a foot in order to drive a big foot into the crimson stained face that stared up from the dusty earth. Not a moment too soon, Montgomery rolled clear of the kick as he scrambled to his feet. Each man moved in to close the gap between them so they could resume the raging battle.

Crenshaw connected with a left-right combination that brought a stream of crimson from Montgomery's battered nose. The blows did not slow the red-headed scholar down. The professor's left jab popped out once, twice, three times to smash the lips of his opponent before swinging a hard right hook that opened a terrible gash above the giant's left eye. Scarlet flowed freely into the man's eye, so he pawed at his face attempting to clear his vision. Instead of retreating, the outlaw fired off a right that pounded the Easterner's ear, then followed this with a left that rocked Montgomery's head in the opposite direction. Quickly, the red head faked a left to the man's good eye, then unleashed a right that landed square on Crenshaw's left temple. Eyes glassy, the big man swayed upon his feet. Without delay the professor swung a big right to Jasper's jaw that struck home with an ear-splitting crack. The bandit crumpled to the earth in a heap of jumbled arms and legs. Montgomery turned toward the others with a sheepish grin animating his bloody, battered features.

'We did try to warn you,' Robertson spoke up as his colleague gulped air into his lungs. The little professor had maneuvered behind Alfred Crenshaw so the little .41 calibre pistol pressed against the back of the man's head. Everyone's eyes had been riveted upon the fistic battle, but attention now shifted to the other Cranshaw held captive by the bird-like Professor Robertson. 'It was not our desire to resort to violence, but you gentlemen left us with no alternatives.'

'Quite right.' Montgomery shook his red, freckled head in agreement as he used a handkerchief to clean his face. 'Quite right, Professor Robertson.'

'Now that Professor Montgomery has demonstrated our determination in this matter,' Robertson continued, 'I'm afraid I will have to insist that you gentlemen move along. You can load this unfortunate casualty upon his horse,' he nodded toward the fallen figure of Jasper Crenshaw, 'and then leave us alone.'

West and Russell lowered their hands, but seemed unsure of the situation at hand. Neither wanted to make any move that would push the tense situation in the direction of further violence for fear that the Easterners could be killed. Malone and Holt stood stunned and obviously confused over the odd turn of events. Each of the outlaws held their hands near the grips of the pistols strapped about their waists. The silver-haired gunman and the old trapper surveyed the scene with caution. Their concern remained the welfare of the eccentric scholars who now seemed in control.

'Indeed,' Montgomery echoed, having caught his breath by now, 'it is time for you to move along without any further delays or discussion.'

Malone allowed a nasty grin to emerge as his confidence returned. 'You boys don't really think we're gonna let you scare us off with that little pop gun, do you?'

'We ain't even sure you know how to use that thing,' Holt sneered at the professors with unconcealed contempt.

'Oh I can use this weapon at least as well as Professor Montgomery uses his fists,' Robertson replied with absolute seriousness, 'and certainly well enough to eliminate your companion here.' He referred to Alfred Crenshaw with the bore of the .41 derringer.

'Make no mistake, gentlemen,' Montgomery voiced support for his colleague, 'if anyone makes a threatening move, then Professor Robertson will be forced to pull that trigger on your friend.'

'Ain't no friend of mine,' Malone growled as his hand grabbed for the big Remington .44 holstered upon his right hip. 'Get 'em, Len!'

Holt took the cue from the one-eyed bad-man. His two hands swept downward rapidly. As Malone's fingers gripped the .44, Holt already had the short-barrelled twin .45 Colts out and levelled. Both pistols belched lead as the little gunman squeezed triggers. He put two shots into Alfred Crenshaw before the boss outlaw's pistol cleared leather. Alfred jerked spasmodically as the lead ploughed into his chest. Crimson made a nasty stain upon the man's soiled plaid shirt. He fell forward to land upon his face in the rocky soil with a resounding thud. He never twitched or moved again.

BOOM! BOOM!

Len Holt came to an abrupt halt as he twisted to face the silver-haired gunman whose smoking Colt Navy .36 had sounded in sudden explosions in the warm, spring afternoon. Attempting to bring his .45 pistols to bear upon the big shootist, the outlaw gunman found that his hands simply grew numb, so the matching Colt Revolvers slipped from his grasp to fall to the earth near his feet. Holt sat down hard to stare at the puddle of scarlet that leaked from the two holes near the centre of his own shirt front.

Meanwhile, Malone, confused over which direction he should direct his own fire, had finally decided upon Russell as his target. Never a fast draw, Russell's advanced years had slowed him even further. The old man seemed almost to move in slow motion bringing the ornate Smith and Wesson American .44 from the holster at his hip. The big pistol cleared leather smoothly and the old scout had begun to raise the weapon when he saw that it was too late.

BOOM!

One shot. The lead punched a neat, black hole upon entering the skull, but exited through a cavity the size of a small fist on the other side. Russell looked on with amazement as Bad Eye Bill Malone tightly clutched his Remington revolver while falling forward in a large pile of loose limbs. Then movement caught the corner of his eye.

BOOM!

A final shot. This one from Russell's .44. One shot to the head of Jasper Crenshaw, who had been struggling to pull a well-used revolver from his pocket. Briefly forgotten in the gun battle, the battered outlaw had regained consciousness in time to die. Russell struck the big pistol back in the holster.

'I might be a bit slow,' he spoke with grim satisfaction, 'but I still hit what I aim fer.' He turned and directed his gaze at the Easterners who stood across the shallow pit in silence. 'Milly and Tilly, thanks! You done good, boys!'

For once, Robertson and Montgomery were speechless. The little professor stood with the smoking derringer in his right fist. He had, of course, managed to shoot the outlaw boss just before the killer had pulled the trigger on Russell. The big red head only nodded in response to the mountain man's expression of appreciation.

'Looks to me like that 'un is dead.' Russell jerked a thumb at Alfred Crenshaw, who lay in a sticky pool of crimson. 'Shot down by that little snake of a gunfighter jist 'cause he was in the way.'

'Malone's dead for sure,' West spoke quietly as he stepped toward the fallen form of Len Holt. 'I ain't sure about this one.'

'Not yet,' Holt's voice emerged as barely more than a whisper, 'Never thought it would end like this.'

'Nobody ever does, son.' West was gentle as he knelt beside the dying man. Holt now lay stretched out amidst the sage and yucca that dotted the canyon floor.

'I knew you was good.' Holt coughed weakly. 'I saw you in that saloon the other night.'

'I'm good enough,' the old gunman replied.

'Who are you?'

'Just an old man who wants to be left alone.'

'You got to be somebody...' Holt's voice

trailed off as he struggled with the words.

'I ain't nobody.' West shook his head in sad resignation as the other man's eyes closed for a final time. 'Just a hardware store man from Spit Junction.'

TEN

The remainder of the afternoon passed in relative quiet as Russell, West, and the professors dug shallow graves for the four badmen, then piled stone and broken rock upon them to keep the coyotes away from the remains. Robertson and Montgomery had insisted upon a decent burial for the outlaws. Russell and West had agreed due to the practical necessity of removing the bodies from the excavation site and putting the dead bandits under ground to hold the stench of death at bay from their work area. They would have to remain in this vicinity so the Easterners could complete their work among the mastodon's bones. No one needed to be reminded of the grim show-down now only a few hours past. Dried, black stains upon the rocky earth, and the tight knots in hungry bellies were reminders enough.

Professors Robertson and Montgomery found some solace in the beauty of Palo Duro Canyon. The setting sun brought a repeat performance of the dawn's colourful display. The canyon's walls seemed to dance in shades of red, orange, brown, and grey. Russell prepared an evening meal after he and West moved their camp the short distance to the excavation site. As the bright orange globe sank beneath the rocky canyon rim, the old mountain man squared his shoulders to call out for attention.

'Enough of this dagblasted silence!' the trapper roared out in his gravelly voice. 'Everybody git your mangy hides over to the fire fer supper. We got buffler steaks and taters along with the finest biscuits and gravy west of the Mississippi. Git it now or go hungry fer the night!'

'On our way, Mr Russell.' Robertson forced a smile as he struggled to his feet and made his way to the roaring blaze of a camp fire.

'We wouldn't miss one of your delicious meals.' Montgomery's grin was genuine as he let a pink tongue moisten dry lips in anticipation of the thick buffalo steak with all the trimmings.

'Dish it up, old man.' Elijah West settled himself across the fire from his wiry companion as Three Toes began to pass the plates piled high with steaming meat, potatoes, biscuits, and thick, dark gravy. Without a doubt, the foursome were in for yet another grand feast. As they ate, tensions melted, and West posed the question that had nagged at him throughout the late afternoon.

'Professors.' The silver-haired gunman spoke softly, but he attracted the Easterners' attention. Both men's spirits seemed considerably revived now as they enjoyed their meal along with the warmth of the yellow blaze. 'I ain't meanin' to pry, but I was wonderin' just how it was that you two college gentlemen could put up such a scrap against them fellers this afternoon. I mean,' he eyed the odd couple with curiosity, 'you don't really strike me as the rough and tumble type.'

'Blazes!' the old scout exclaimed. 'I'm glad you asked 'em that one. I've been about to burst! Milly and Tilly here have taken everything that's been throwed at 'em without so much as the flutter of an eyelash then all the sudden they's like wildcats in a burlap bag. What's the story, boys?'

'No real story gentlemen,' Robertson responded with a sheepish grin enlivening his features. 'Professor Montgomery here was the champion of his college boxing team and has always managed to keep his hand in over the years by training the young men at school.'

'While Professor Robertson,' Montgomery interjected, 'has been the top pistol marksman at our college and the surrounding county for more than twenty years of exhibitions and contests.'

'You birds take the cake.' Russell wiped gravy from his beard with the back of a leathery claw. 'But why didn't you fellers fight back afore this? What was you waitin' on afore you bared your claws to strike back?'

'That's an easy one, Mr Russell.' Robertson met the trapper's green eyes with sincerity. 'You and Mr West were in danger.'

'We had no choice except to take action, or you might have been killed.' Montgomery looked across the fire's blaze at the blue eyes of Elijah West. 'Harm to either of you was simply an unacceptable alternative.'

'Milly and Tilly,' Russell's tone remained steady, but filled with strong sentiment, 'I jist want you to know that I appreciate what you done. This old hide ain't worth much, but I been wearing it a long time. I've grown kinda fond of it after all these years; thanks, boys!'

'Thank you, professors.' West joined his own simple words of appreciation with those of his companion's. 'You saved this old man's bacon for sure.'

'You are certainly welcome, gentlemen.' The bird-like head bobbed up and down with enthusiasm. 'Please, think no more about it.'

'Certainly, my dear friends.' The freckled face beamed as Montgomery scratched at wiry, red hair. 'There's no need to give it another thought.'

'By the way,' West shifted the topic of conversation with a casual grin 'you gents might not know it, but there's been a government reward out on that payroll for years now. If I recollect correctly,' he paused for a moment with all eyes upon him, 'we each stand to bring in about five hundred dollars as our share in recovering that box of loot.'

'You ain't joshing an old man are you, boy?' Russell looked at his friend with a hint of suspicion in his eyes. 'That's a pocket full fer this old mountain goat.'

'No,' the gunman shook his head, 'this is no joke. We each ought to collect five hundred as our share of that government reward for bringing in this old stolen payroll. That should keep your belly full through the winter.'

The sombre mood that had gripped the camp earlier was now completely dispersed by this exchange. Normal conversation resumed. In spite of the violent afternoon, the outlaws had met only with the harsh frontier justice they so richly deserved, and, after all, the professors had uncovered a tremendous archaeological find in the bones of the prehistoric mastodon. The Easterners chattered in an almost endless stream of scholarly jargon for the next hour as each completed his meal, then cleaned up the camp site in preparation for sleep. At last, the exhausted professors settled into their blankets for the evening. Steady breathing indicated they were quickly sound asleep.

'Got a little something in my saddlebags,'

West offered up with a wink in the direction of his old partner. 'I'll be right back.'

'I'll git the mugs, Elijah.' Russell's lips turned up in a grin almost hidden among the bushy grey beard that surrounded it. 'I was hoping you brung along the dessert.'

Within moments, the shootist had returned with a half full bottle of Tennessee whiskey. He splashed a generous helping into each of the battered tin mugs held out by the mountain man before pounding the cork back into the bottle neck with the heel of his calloused hand. After accepting the cup offered by his friend, he settled down by the fire to share the whiskey and conversation with his companion. They each tasted the fine bourbon with satisfaction. Then West broke the brief silence by giving voice to the nagging question that had eaten away at him over the past few days.

'You reckon they can keep their mouths shut about me?' He indicated the sleeping Easterners with a nod of his silver head. 'I got a new name and a new life back in Spit

Junction. I really don't want to give it up.'

'They'll keep it to themselves, son.' Russell nodded his head in solemn assurance. 'Don't fret over it fer a minute. Them boys is mighty peculiar what with all their fancy talk about elephink bones and sich as that, but they's all right. You can trust 'em both to keep it all quiet.'

'That's good.' The big gunman smiled gently. 'I got no use for the shootin' and killin' any more, Three Toes. I ain't lookin' to step back into the wild life. Crazy as it might sound to you,' he sipped the whiskey with a whispered slurping sound, 'I'm proud of my little hardware store, and I like livin' the quiet life there in town.'

'You like more'n that store, son.' The grizzled old man grinned wide in the fire light as he gulped another mouthful of the whiskey. 'You like that little school teacher gal.' He held up a leather-tough palm to silence the protests of his long-time partner. 'Now, don't start it up with me, boy. I been around a spell and knowed you longer than anybody left out here on the frontier. You got a stirrin' in your heart fer that woman. No point in denying it, Elijah.'

A long minute of silence passed as Elijah West sipped at the bourbon whiskey in deep thoughtfulness. 'So what if I do,' he shrugged his broad shoulders. 'You think Miss Berry'd be interested in a broke down old gun fighter such as me? You think I'd stand a chance with a woman like that?'

'Son,' a faint smile played among the grey whiskers, 'you ain't never gonna know the answer to that lessen you court the gal.' His grin quickly faded as the trapper turned serious for a moment. 'I believe I saw the spark in her eyes when she looked at you in the store the other day, but who knows the secret to a woman's love? There jist ain't no figgerin' them women; that's a fact.' Russell looked up from his cup to stare deep into his friend's blue eyes. 'This here's fer certain though; if you don't even make the effort, then you'll never know fer sure. Don't end up wishin' and wonderin'; just git yourself hitched up to that school teacher so I can have me a baby to bounce on my knee next time I'm through this old Texas Panhandle.'

West returned the smile that now split the old man's shaggy whiskers. They each re-filled the cups to have a final drink before crawling into warm bedrolls stretched out beside the glowing coals of the camp fire. A good night's rest would make everyone feel better.

Eleven days later found everyone safe and happy back in the little town of Spit Junction. Professors Robertson and Mont-gomery had completed their excavation. Then West had retuned to town to bring pack horses along with assistance in the form of a drifter and a couple of hard luck locals who needed some temporary work. Under the watchful eyes of the Easterners, these men had crated the prehistoric fossils with care, then loaded the pack animals to transport the bones back to Spit Junction. From there, the odd couple arranged for the crates to be shipped home to Hopkins College in Howardville, Maine. The college professors seemed none the worse for wear in spite of their violent adventures and incredible physical labours. They remained in delightful good humour as they renewed their acquaintance with the fiery rotgut whiskey at the Emerald Palace Saloon.

The Irish barkeep, O'Cooners, poured another round for the professors from his special 'house brand' and produced the finest Tennessee bourbon whiskey which he kept on hand especially for the local hardware store owner, Joshua Easterly. With all glasses full, the bartender placed the bottles upon the small corner table for the enjoyment of the four men who now relaxed in the friendly tavern. 'Sure and now it's good to have you back, Mr Easterly.' He spoke with a wink and a grin to the big silver-haired gunman. 'We've missed you around here to be sure.'

'Good to be back.' West raised the glass in salute before sipping the amber liquid with relish. 'I'll be open for business again in the mornin'.'

'To be sure' the Irishman smiled as he paced back to the scarred wooden counter. His feet scattered clean sawdust in his path. 'To be sure,' he repeated.

'You git that reward business all settled?' Three Toes posed his question with a raised eyebrow, then followed it with a mouthful of West's bourbon. 'Is we gonna git that five hunnerd a piece you was talkin' about?'

'It's on the way.' West simply smiled before taking a small sip of whiskey. 'You'll be dangerous with that much money in your pocket.' The men at the table laughed as Russell glared at his friend in mock anger. Then the scout's face took on a mischievous grin as he shifted the topic of conversation.

'I didn't see you aroun' here today, son,' the old trapper spoke with a twinkle in his meadow-green eyes. 'Where'd you git off to all day in a little town sich as this here one?'

'Since when do I have to answer to you, old man?' The shootist grinned as his face flushed pink. 'If it's any of your business, I took a certain lady on a long picnic.' West and Russell chuckled softly as their eyes locked across the table. 'I feel the magic.' He tapped his chest with two fingers just above his heart.

'Treat her good, son,' the scout's face beamed his happiness, 'she's a keeper fer sure.'

'Have you informed Mr Easterly of our news?' Robertson used the gunman's assumed name. He and Montgomery had sworn secrecy regarding the hardware store owner's true identity. Now the little professor glowed with good will as he and his companion knocked back another jolt of the fiery red whiskey with no discernible effect. 'Does he know of our plans?'

'Indeed,' Montgomery added in their typical pattern of conversation, 'you really must pass along our exciting proposal for adventure.'

'What's this all about?' The man known as Joshua Easterly shot a curious glance at his old friend. 'I thought you were set on stickin' here with me for a spell. Last time we talked on the subject, you was gonna give them old bones a rest here in Spit Junction. Maybe help out around the store for the winter.'

'Hell, son,' Russell scratched idly at the bushy grey whiskers that covered his face. 'Ain't no call fer me to sit aroun' some dagblasted town sich as this here. That ain't fer me and we both know it.' He let his meadow-green eyes meet the sky-blue ones of his friend. 'Besides all that, I got me a home up north in the mountains, and Milly and Tilly here have done give me another job.'

'That is a certain fact,' Robertson grinned as he gulped yet another mouthful of O'Cooner's wicked whiskey. 'We have in our possession another map.'

'This one will take us north to the red rock country of northern Wyoming.' Montgomery smiled brightly in anticipation of the new expedition. 'We are eager to be on our way with Mr Russell as our guide.'

West shook his head in amused disbelief as he looked from the faces of the professors to that of his old partner. 'And you're gonna head north with 'em to look fer more old bones?'

'Don't see why not,' the old man bristled. 'It's on my way home to the high country of the Montana Territory.' He winked a green eye at his companion. 'I might as well git paid fer baby sittin' with Milly and Tilly here as travel it by my lonesome.'

'You got your little pistol handy, Professor Robertson?' West asked with a mock serious expression to his features. 'Your fists primed and ready for action, Professor Mont-gomery?' Each man gulped as they drained another round of whiskey with obvious enjoyment. They nodded their heads in affirmative responses.

William Russell stared across the table at Elijah West with unconcealed curiosity. 'What you concerned about all that fer, son? I got all my weapons.' He indicated the pistol, knife, and tomahawk at his belt as well as the big Henry rifle propped within easy reach in the corner. 'Besides,' the scout shrugged his buckskin clad shoulders, 'there ain't no danger jist lookin' fer them old rocky fossil critters.'

'Everywhere you three go,' West raised his glass of Tennessee whiskey in salute to the others at the table, 'seems you find trouble in the form of bones, bullets, and badmen.'

All present broke out in roaring laughter before drinking deeply in good fellowship and warm friendship. Life was good for the four friends who shared a table in a final evening together. The Emerald Palace Saloon rang with the sounds of good humour while thoughts of the future shone brightly, even through the smoky haze of the small tavern.

'Then let's drink another round,' Russell wiped at his mouth with the palm of a claw-like hand before raising his glass in another toast, 'to bones, bullets, and badmen.'

And they did. All night long.

The publishers hope that this book has given you enjoyable reading. Large Print Books are especially designed to be as easy to see and hold as possible. If you wish a complete list of our books please ask at your local library or write directly to:

Dales Large Print Books
Magna House, Long Preston,
Skipton, North Yorkshire.
BD23 4ND